THE DEADLIES

SPIDERS ON THE CASE

The author gratefully acknowledges Dr. Greta Binford, Professor of Biology at
Lewis & Clark College, for her help with the spider research in this book.

This book was originally published in hardcover by
Scholastic Press in 2011.

ISBN 978-0-545-11731-9

12 11 10 9 8 7 6 5 4 3 2 1   11 12 13 14 15 16/0
Printed in the U.S.A.   40
First Scholastic paperback printing, December 2011

THE DEADLIES

SPIDERS ON THE CASE

by **KATHRYN LASKY**

illustrated by **STEPHEN GILPIN**

SCHOLASTIC INC.

New York   Toronto   London   Auckland
Sydney   Mexico City   New Delhi   Hong Kong

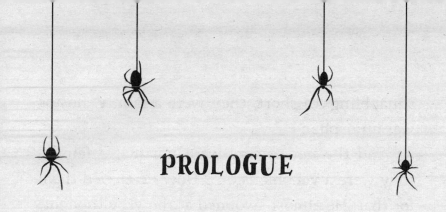

PROLOGUE

In the dim light of the rare books room of the Boston Public Library, a brown walnut spider, a type of orb weaver, waited in a shimmering silken web stretched between two ancient volumes of Greek poetry. The young spider had been secretly observing the new spider family since their arrival almost two weeks before. The mother and three spiderlings were everything he had ever dreamed of being. Charming and smart, they spun stories as easily as silk. Behind their three pairs of eyes, they had little fiddle markings. Buster himself — for that was the brown walnut spider's name — had no such interesting marks. In addition to all this, the three spiderlings were curious, lively, and often squabbling. In short, they were a family. Buster was an orphan.

And the newcomers were not just a family, they were a venomous one. How he envied them for that. He almost swooned at the very thought. And he needed their venom desperately. For something very bad was happening in the Boston Public Library, and it had to be stopped. The little spider family was clueless as to what was going on practically in front of their very eyes — all twenty-four of them! But with this family on his side, the horrid crime spree would end!

ONE
Squabbling Spiders

And when Madame unfolded the gown from the layers of tissue paper, she almost fainted with delight at Monsieur Poulet's creation. "Monsieur!" she exclaimed. "It is too beautiful — *trop belle*. It is a chef d'oeuvre, a masterpiece." Jo Bell hesitated over the next words. "It shimmers like the clouds with just a soupçon of" — Jo Bell paused — "soupçon. I think that means 'a hint.' Yes, a hint of silver thread. I love the word 'soupçon'!" Jo Bell exclaimed, and looked up at her mother. "Mom, have you heard anything I've said in the last five minutes?"

"What, dear? Something about soup's on. Yes, a lovely human expression for 'dinner is ready.'"

Jo Bell sighed. What did one have to do to get attention in this family? She was the oldest. Didn't she deserve a little respect? Instead, everyone fussed over Felix and the "enchanting" webs he spun. Their mother had called his last one a "triumph." She wanted to shout, "Hello! I'm here, too, you know! *MOI!*" But her mother only had eyes for Felix.

"'Soupçon' — it's the French word for 'hint.' Mom, you're not listening to me! I've been teaching myself French. And look, I spun a replica of the very gown Madame Gerora described. I copied it from the book I was telling you about."

"Oh, yes, oh, yes," her mother replied somewhat vaguely. "Well, that's very nice, dear. Quite lovely."

Jo Bell's mom's enthusiasm meter seemed to hover around a five as opposed to the solid ten with bells and whistles it reached for Felix's masterpieces.

"You call that art?" Felix said, examining the gown Jo Bell had just spun.

"I certainly do!" Jo Bell replied, crossing her front legs in annoyance. "You are not the only artist in the family, you know, Felix. Fashion is art, especially high fashion. You don't know everything," Jo Bell huffed.

Sock it to him, Jo Bell, Buster thought.

"I know it's not as good as this new web design of mine. It's perfect for trapping and storing silverfish. Elegant yet practical. Form follows function, as the great architects say."

"Now, Felix, mind your manners. We can't all be architects as you are." Edith, the spiderlings' mother, swung down from the web repair work she was tending in the corner.

"Mom, this is beyond manners! He is insulting what I care about."

"All he said was that fashion isn't an art form, dear."

"Mom, now you — you're saying it, too!" Jo Bell was ready to explode. Her mother always sided with Felix.

"It is a kind of art, dear!"

Kind of. Two little words that made fashion design sound like a half art at best! Her mother's lukewarm defense only made Jo Bell angrier.

"Fashion is so . . . so . . . vain. It's really a frivolous preoccupation of humans," Felix added.

WHAT?! Was Felix the only one who got credit for anything? Jo Bell felt like an alien in her own family. She thought, *That's exactly it. I might as well be a Peruvian jumping spider or a Mexican lace weaver.*

Trying her best not to explode with anger, Jo Bell said with all the patience she could muster, "Mom, I take offense that you feel my interest is a 'kind of' art form, but I can definitely tell you that French is certainly not a 'kind of' language."

"Oh, dear, oh, dear." Edith was beginning to wring two of her rear legs together. In another few seconds, she'd be wringing six of her eight legs. "I didn't mean that at all, Jo Bell. I misspoke. Since we've been here in the Boston Public

Library, we have all learned so much already. You especially, dear. Some French! And now Felix is trying as well."

"What about à la mode?" Julep asked. She was the youngest of the family and just returning from one of her explorations in the pop-up books section of the Rare Books Department. "Isn't that the one with ice cream or something? A gown with ice cream. Yum."

"No, darling, that is just a food term for the most part — although, loosely translated, it can mean 'in style.'" Edith paused. "Let's stop the bickering. We promised Fatty that we would meet him at the theater this afternoon for the matinee of the flamenco dancers. Another lovely art form that we can explore."

Fat Cat, or Fatty, was the godspider of Edith's children. He had traveled with them to Boston all the way from the philharmonic hall in Los Angeles. But Fatty preferred theatrical settings to libraries.

"I'm not going," Jo Bell said stubbornly.

"Now, Jo Bell, don't be that way." Edith sighed.

"What way? Not 'gifted' like Felix?" Jo Bell's mother was always talking about how gifted Felix was ever since he had begun spinning beautiful new webs that usually only orb weaver spiders could create. Here, Jo Bell had taught herself French and spun the lovely design of an evening gown, but did her mother say anything? Once more she asked herself, what did one have to do to be noticed in this family?

"Suit yourself, dear," said Edith. "If you prefer to stay here."

"That's exactly what I'll do," Jo Bell replied. She was furious. Ever since Felix's accident at the philharmonic hall in Los Angeles, where he lost a leg, Edith had been fawning over him. But for silk's sake, the leg had grown back, as it usually did with young spiders!

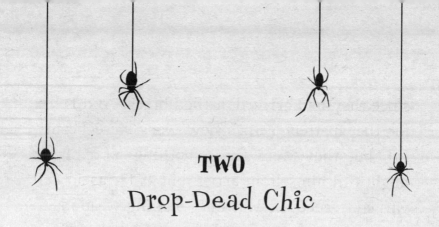

TWO
Drop-Dead Chic

Jo Bell settled in between her favorite pages of a book, *Les Dessins des Hauts Couturiers*. She had finally figured out what the French title meant. The book was a bound portfolio of original fashion drawings by famous French designers, including Coco Chanel and the legendary Charles Worth. There were even drawings by the woman who designed Marie Antoinette's ball gowns. But did anyone give her credit for learning French? No! All they could talk about was how stupid fashion was!

And what was so fabulous about hanging out in a pop-up circus? That was where Jo Bell's younger sister, Julep, had ensconced herself since they had arrived at the library. And Felix, for that matter? Felix's new webs were beautiful, but they were traps, nothing more. Felix might call himself an artist, but as far as Jo Bell was concerned, he was only making weapons to catch silverfish, book mites, and the rest of the bugs eating up volumes in the rare books room. Lately, he had buried himself in military history. It was interesting, but what made reading about war any better than learning French?

Forget about them, she told herself. She wanted to look at this gorgeous drawing of a dress from more than a hundred years ago. It had a bunched-up funny thing on the back called a bustle. Jo Bell caught a glimpse of herself reflected in a glass case. *I have a natural bustle*, she thought.

All spiders did, for that matter. A spider's body contained two major parts — the front and the back. The front had the head, the back the stomach. The head was quite tiny when compared to the back end, which swelled up somewhat like a bustle. Now, if Jo Bell could only spin herself a bit of silk, not for a web but for a spider-size gown that would flow out over her natural bustle!

Just as she was having these thoughts, she heard voices.

"Oh, hello, Ms. Smoot. It's been a while."

"Yes, I know."

"Your husband was in a few days ago. So good to see you."

It was Tom the conservator speaking. He welcomed everyone to the rare books room so warmly — even a family of extremely venomous brown recluse spiders. Jo Bell would never forget how Edith had told them to freeze when they first spotted Tom. But what did Tom do? Squash them under his rather large foot? Shriek and faint as the conductor at the philharmonic hall had done when he saw Felix on his baton? Call the dreaded E-Men, the exterminators? No! Nothing of the kind. He had merely bent over and whispered, "Welcome! I am so glad to see you. They tell me that book lice are quite tasty — from a spider's point of view. There are plenty here. They eat paper. You will be doing a great service to the rare books collection if you would indulge yourself."

And the book lice were tasty and the spider family did indulge. Edith insisted. If Tom was kind enough to allow them to live in the magnificent Boston Public Library, they must earn their keep. Within a day of their arrival, Edith had organized patrols to hunt down the little critters. And it was not just book lice but silverfish and cockroaches and beetles who bored, gnawed, and feasted on some of the world's oldest and most treasured books. In the dim, soft glow of the rare books room, a great battle raged — the battle to preserve priceless volumes from enemies like dampness, mold, and bugs!

Jo Bell heard Ms. Smoot sigh with pleasure as she opened the fashion journal she had been exploring. Then the woman whispered, "These bustles will make the ultimate fashion statement in my new collection! They're drop-dead chic!"

Suddenly, a long, sharp shadow fell across the beautiful drawing. It wasn't a pencil. It was a blade! Jo Bell dived into the gutter of the book. Then came a tiny rasping *swizzz* and Jo Bell felt the page shake. A small jolt sent her deeper

into the gutter until she fell through a tiny hole in the book's binding, thankfully safe from the sharp edge of the blade. Before her eyes — all six of them — the page with the beautiful illustration of the bustles vanished. It was gone in the blink of her half dozen eyes (had those eyes possessed eyelids to blink).

"Toodle-oo!" Ms. Smoot trilled into the conservator's room, where Tom was restoring a diary of John Adams, the second president of the United States.

"Good-bye, Ms. Smoot."

Jo Bell lay in the binding, stunned. Did Tom realize what had just taken place? How could she tell him? Although Jo Bell's family understood English, they couldn't speak to humans, and humans couldn't understand spiders at all. And to think that her mother believed that silverfish were the bad guys in the library! The glint of the blade in Agnes Smoot's hand flashed in Jo Bell's mind like a bad dream that wouldn't go away.

THREE
Terminally Shy

What is she going to do? Buster wondered. *Will she panic? Naw! Why would she? She's got venom!* But Buster could tell that the spider girl was shocked. *Well, get used to it*, he thought. Agnes Smoot and her husband, Eldridge Montague, were becoming bolder with each theft. What a team they made! Eldridge was a dealer in old maps, and beneath her ugly wig and horn-rimmed glasses, Agnes was none other than the new rising design star Diane de Funk. "Where does she get her ideas?" people marveled. Where indeed! She sliced the pages out of old books and magazines and even lifted original drawings and sketches from the portfolios of some of the world's finest designers, all from the rare books room of this grand old library. But now, with the arrival of some of the most deadly spiders on earth, there was hope. The destruction of priceless treasures from the Rare Books Department could be stopped. And the wondrous newcomers were a family!

Buster had no recollection of his parents or even of any sisters or brothers. He had hatched in the Boston Public Library. To be specific, his hatching occurred in the armpit of a statue of a shepherd boy playing the flute. Buster imagined

that his mother had deposited her egg sac there because (1) she was a sculptor herself. (2) She might have been a musician. (3) Or a shepherd? (4) Or maybe she just liked armpits.

It was a boring location, for no music came out of the flute, and sheep did not frequent the Boston Public Library. So Buster decided to move on. His next place of residence was the Bates Hall reading room of the library. When he crept into that vast space lit by hundreds of green-lamp-shaded table lights, he thought he had landed on another planet.

The green glow hovered over the oak tables like a cloud of the most exotic butterflies. A hush enveloped the huge room, and Buster felt smarter simply walking into it. It was in Bates Hall that Buster educated himself by perching on the shoulders of unsuspecting readers or nestling in the gutters of their open books. The one advantage of being a walnut orb weaver was that Buster was very flat and a boring brown. He was able to squeeze into the smallest places without being noticed. There was no spider in the world better at pretending to be dead than a walnut orb weaver. Buster could drop like a stone from his web and remain motionless for a long, long time with his legs tucked up, until any danger had passed. But could he deliver a fierce sting? Never. He had no hope of stopping Agnes and Eldridge on his own.

Now this lovely toxic family had arrived. They had been wonderful in apprehending silverfish and beetles and all manner of insects that were chomping through the books. The mother organized night patrols and was constantly sending her children out on recon missions. They had discovered a breeding community of little paper sharks on their first night and had finished them off by dawn. But there was bigger prey — humans bent on destruction.

Unfortunately, Buster lacked not only venom but nerve. He was painfully shy. Was he supposed to waltz up to this nice young girl —

who was just about his age — and say, *Please join me on a mission to stop two dangerous criminals who might squash us both*? For silk's sake, he didn't even have the guts to say hello! His social skills were zero.

Buster couldn't remember how many self-help books he had read about how to make friends and influence people. He figured human advice would work for spiders, but he just couldn't get up the nerve.

He had to do something, though, and soon. Agnes Smoot was growing bolder.

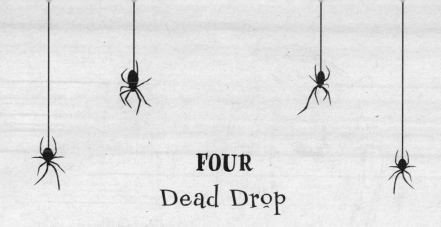

FOUR
Dead Drop

Jo Bell made her way back to the glass case that displayed some of the library's oldest books — those printed before the year 1501 — slightly dazed from what she had just witnessed. She comforted herself with the musty smell of old parchment and the familiar sound of Tom Parker on the telephone. "Yes, we do have a first edition of the Champollion dictionary of hieroglyphs. It happens to be my area of interest. So, yes, we have quite a bit on hieroglyphics here. 'Hieroglyphics are us,' you might say." He chuckled at his little joke.

"What's this?" Jo Bell muttered. Something had fallen directly in Jo Bell's path, like a flake of peeling paint from the ceiling. She peered at it.

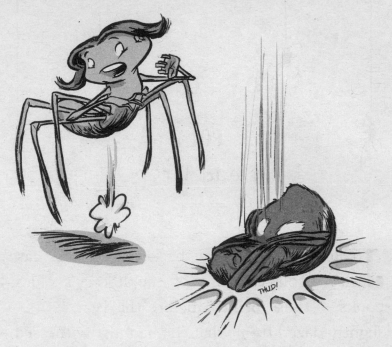

I cannot believe I'm doing this, Buster thought. *Pretending I'm dead so I can meet a girl! How pathetic can you get?*

Jo Bell crouched down on her eight legs to look at him closely. "It's not dust," she whispered.

Right! Right! I'm not dust, Buster thought.

"Not a flake of paint." Jo Bell spoke softly.

"Are you kidding?" Buster squealed. "Paint! Who would ever paint something this dingy brown?"

"Yikes!" Jo Bell squealed. "It's talking."

"Oh! Oh! I didn't mean to scare you. It just slipped out." Buster was now in the process of unpacking his legs, which had been tucked in so tightly that there had not been the least hint that he had one leg, let alone eight. Jo Bell was astonished.

"Uh . . . this is sort of hard to explain," Buster said.

"Well, do try. Have you been here all along? I mean since my family arrived?"

"Yes, yes indeed."

"How come you never said anything? Not even a how-do-ya-do!"

"I . . . I . . . I have social issues," Buster stammered. Then he blurted out, "Shy! I'm shy!"

"You mean you've just watched us and never said a word?"

Buster nodded.

"That's like spying!"

"Oh, no, please don't say that! I mean I . . . I didn't have anything bad in mind." He paused.

"Well, actually, I sort of did, but not bad for you."

"Bad for who?" Jo Bell whispered. She was suddenly frightened.

Buster picked up on it immediately. "Don't be scared. I couldn't hurt a fly. That's my problem. I have no venom! But you saw what happened back there when you were in the fashion portfolio."

"You saw that, too?"

"I did. And it's not the first time. And her husband is even worse. He's cut out at least half a dozen old maps — the latest one of Virginia drawn by the explorer John Smith in 1612."

"No!" Jo Bell exclaimed.

"Yes!"

"And Tom doesn't know about it?"

"No, and believe me, I have tried to get his attention. But I don't know how."

"Yes," Jo Bell said thoughtfully. Communication with humans was always a problem. "So what do you suggest?"

"Well — just a little nip, a teensy-weensy bit of venom — a soupçon, as the French would say?" Buster spoke in a somewhat quavery voice while shifting his weight nervously from one of his eight legs to another and another and another.

"No! The French would NOT say that! There is no such thing as a soupçon of our venom. It's totally toxic no matter what the amount. Powerful, potent, and disastrous for human beings!" Jo Bell screeched.

Buster's request went against everything Edith had ever taught her family. You didn't attack something you couldn't eat.

Jo Bell took a deep breath. "I have to tell you — by the way, what is your name?"

"Buster. What's yours?" He only asked to be polite. He knew Jo Bell's name but didn't want her to think he had been spying. Even if he had sort of peeked in on the family from time to time.

"Jo Bell. But as I was saying, Buster, this is

not a good idea. In fact, it is a horrible idea. Period!"

"But they are destroying the treasures of this library."

"Do you know what happens when brown recluses are discovered?"

"No, what?"

"E-Men come."

"E-Men? What are you talking about?"

"Obviously being a nontoxic, venomless spider, you don't know of such things."

Now Buster was cringing with shame. "Don't rub it in. It's not my fault. I was born this way."

"I'm not saying it is your fault. But if you were toxic, you would realize that as soon as brown recluses are discovered, the exterminators come. And believe me, their poison is worse than ours. We'll be dead. You, too!"

"But Tom loves us. Loves all of us."

"Tom will have nothing to say in the matter if someone gets bitten. The exterminators will be called. And trust me, we don't want that. My family has spent the better part of our lives on the run."

"So you're saying a quick little bite is not an option?"

"You can bet every one of your eight legs it isn't!"

"Hmmm," Buster said softly. "I guess we'll just have to think of something else."

"What do you mean 'we'?" Jo Bell asked suspiciously.

"You and me. Don't you think we could work together?"

"How?"

"We'll just have to think of a way. I don't have venom and you don't think biting is a good idea. But there are other ways."

"Like what?"

"We both spin silk into webs. We have to make a sort of web — a dragnet!" Buster said.

"What's a dragnet?"

"It's a word used by cops. It's like an imaginary net, a web to catch criminals."

"You don't say!" Jo Bell was impressed by Buster's vocabulary and his knowledge. "How do you know all that?"

"I read a lot of crime literature, like Sherlock Holmes, and then some nonfiction books like P. O. Guberhaus's book *Methods of Crime Detection*." Buster named several other books Jo Bell hadn't heard of.

"Well, I'm sure you'll come up with something." Jo Bell began to walk off.

"Wait!" Buster's voice quaked with panic. "Just me?" There was something very pitiful about the way Buster said "just me" that made Jo Bell's spinnerets tingle. "I need your help."

Jo Bell was stunned. *He needs* my *help? He doesn't think I'm vain or just plain silly!* It had been a very long time since anyone had asked for Jo Bell's help.

"Listen, Jo Bell," Buster pleaded. "Just imagine if you and I solve this crime spree. Felix would have to stop picking on you then!"

"So you *were* spying!" So many emotions swirled inside Jo Bell. Spying was nasty, but then again, Buster respected her. Still, what kind of spider spies on another family and doesn't introduce himself? Jo Bell started to walk away again.

"Stop! Come back, please? I just heard them making fun of you, that's all. And it wasn't fair. Not at all."

Jo Bell turned around slowly. Their eyes met, her six and his eight. She looked deeply into the first six, then crept to one side to catch the two extra ones. She peered into their shining darkness. Could he be trusted?

"You really and truly think it wasn't fair? You don't think I'm shallow and frivolous?"

"No, not at all, Jo Bell! You speak French, for silk's sake."

"Really?"

"Jo Bell, it takes all kinds of spiders to make a world, and I think you're one in a million.

Well, to be more precise, one in, say, forty thousand because there are over forty thousand different kinds of spiders."

One in forty thousand, thought Jo Bell. It was music to her ears.

"Just for a second, imagine what your brother would think if you caught two of the worst criminals who ever crossed the threshold of the Boston Public Library. You'd be a hero, not just to your own family but also to the library. To the city of Boston! To the state of Massachusetts. To the United States of America and every person in the world who loves books!"

Jo Bell felt something deep within her begin to glow. *I could be a hero!* she thought. No one would call her shallow or silly or stupid if she caught these terrible humans who were destroying priceless treasures.

"There's just one problem, Buster," Jo Bell said.

"What's that?" he asked.

"No one knows that these crimes against

books are happening, and if no one knows, how will we ever become heroes for solving the crime?"

"Well, for one thing, we don't exactly need to solve it. We know who the criminals are. We could stop it right away. But you don't feel, er . . . uh . . ." Buster hesitated. "You don't think venom is an option?"

This spider needs a wake-up call, Jo Bell thought. "Stop with the venom already, Buster. We never waste venom on something bigger and impossible to digest. And Agnes Smoot is definitely indigestible."

"You have a point. So I guess the real question is, how do we expose the criminals?"

"Yes, that's the question," Jo Bell said.

"We have to figure all this out. But we will, Jo Bell. You and I together. I have great faith in you."

"You do, Buster?" Jo Bell replied. Her voice was soft with wonder.

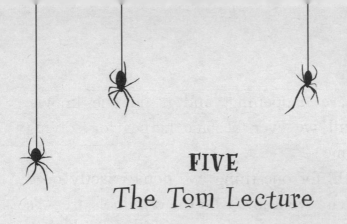

FIVE
The Tom Lecture

Jo Bell returned to the display case. Her head was spinning. Buster had a major self-esteem problem, that was for sure. Although he could deliver a sting, he seemed to believe that just a "touch of the toxic" would help him so much. She had tried to explain how highly overrated venom is.

Buster might not have venom, but he had brains. Jo Bell was tired of Felix being viewed as the only one around with any smarts. So when Buster suggested that they should bring Jo Bell's family into the dragnet, she flatly said no.

"Don't you think your mother should know?"

"Not yet. No one should until we have a plan."

"Well, would you at least introduce me?"

Again, Buster's rather sad voice touched Jo Bell. She wondered if he'd ever had any friends at all. It seemed as if he did nothing but read in between catching the occasional silverfish or cockroach. That was probably why he was so smart.

She agreed to introduce Buster to her family, but she swore him to secrecy about their project. She had been very lucky that her family was gone when she had witnessed Agnes Smoot slicing out that page. This was going to be her case to solve. . . . Well, hers and Buster's.

He had already given her a lengthy reading list of books and magazines about police procedure, from understanding fingerprints to deciphering marks made by shoes in mud. There was no mud in the Boston Public Library, but according to Buster, there were scuff marks on many of the floors.

Most of these books were not in the rare books room. But it was time she visited "the stacks," the library's shadowy back rooms with miles of shelves. And to navigate the stacks, Jo Bell had to learn the Dewey decimal system by which books were classified into subject areas. She must also begin to visit the Bates Hall reading room. Buster was so familiar with the visitors to the reading room that he knew which books they favored. He told her about one elderly woman who loved books on crime and detection. She wore elaborate hats, so it was easy to find a perch and read over her shoulder. Jo Bell couldn't wait to get started.

But now she heard her family returning.

"Hello, dear!" Edith trilled as she skibbled up the leg of the display case where the family web was. "We — well, how should I put it? We had a stimulating time."

"What do you mean?" Jo Bell asked.

"Frankly, I can only take so much flamenco dancing. All that pounding! Clackety-clack with their feet in those chunky shoes! I thought my

spinnerets were going to fall out. It's really too much for a spider my age."

"Oh, Mom!" Felix said. "You'd think you were ancient."

"Well, I'm no spring spider."

"How was Fatty?" Jo Bell asked.

"Quite well, but I think he does miss us. And there is going to be another two weeks of what he calls this 'infernal flamenco.' So he might come for a visit over here. Imagine hearing that six nights a week, and then the matinees on Saturdays and Sundays."

"I made a friend," Jo Bell suddenly blurted out. The announcement was met with stunned silence.

"A friend!" Julep said.

"Not a human, dear? Oh, I hope not. I mean, Tom understands us, but others might . . . might not."

"No, a spider friend," said Jo Bell.

"A spider!" they all said at once.

"One of ours?" Edith asked hopefully. She

would so like to chat with one of their own species.

"No, Mom, not a brown recluse."

"Well, what is she, dear?"

"It's a he, Mom, and he is a walnut orb weaver."

"A *Nuctenea umbratica*," Edith said. "They're a very nice sort. Not venomous, of course."

"Yes, and please don't remind him of that. He has a bit of a self-esteem problem."

"I would, too," Felix said. "I mean, they're orb weavers, but on a scale of zero to ten, their webs are a two, possibly a three, in terms of beauty and elegance."

"Shut up, Felix. He's very nice. He's very shy, he's really smart, and he does not need a critique of his weaving skills from you."

"No squabbling, please, children. Now get ready for night patrol."

"But, Mom," Julep whined. "I'm not even hungry."

"Julep, no whining. I told you not to eat

that cockroach at the theater. It spoiled your appetite."

"But I was hungry then and I'm not hungry now. Besides, I went down to the children's room and they were passing out cookies. There were crumbs all over the place."

"What in the name of silk were you doing down there?"

"Story time. They're reading this great book called *Little House on the Prairie* — all about the pioneer days and this nice little girl named Laura."

"You certainly do flit around," Felix said. "First pop-up circus books and now pioneer books. What will it be next?"

"I'm thinking about Egypt. There's this really cool pop-up book of a pyramid," Julep said.

"I hope it's not in the children's room," Edith said.

"No, it's right here in the rare books. No kids ever come up here! It's one of the antique pop-up books. Actually, they call them movable-parts books. I heard Tom on the phone talking about the pyramid one."

"Well, it's a relief that it's up here. But, Julep, I've said this once and I'll keep saying it until it sinks in."

Jo Bell and Felix exchanged quick glances with their dozen eyes. How often had they heard this lecture?

"Tom Parker is the only human being we have ever met who has welcomed us," Edith began. "He requires nothing of us except that we eat the little pests that are destroying some of the world's greatest treasures. This is our duty not just to Tom but to the reading public. In general I am not fond of humans, but human beings who read improve our planet." She paused. "Is that understood, children?"

Edith's three children bobbed their heads up and down obediently.

She continued, "I think tonight we'll penetrate

the John Adams collection. I heard Tom on the phone today talking about how he was worried about a silverfish invasion. Particularly in those books in Adams's personal collection, where he made notes in the margins."

"Can my friend come, Mom?" Jo Bell asked.

"Oh, your friend — the walnut orb weaver?" Edith asked.

"Buster."

"Buster. Yes, of course, dear. Where is he?"

"Right here," Jo Bell tipped her head toward a crack in the display case.

"Right where?" Julep asked. "I don't see a thing."

"He's shy, very shy." Jo Bell skibbled over to an infinitesimally small crack in the frame of the case. "Buster, come on out and meet the family!" She waited a few seconds. "Come on, Buster."

Slowly, the walnut orb weaver crept out. Edith, Felix, and Julep poked their heads forward. Eighteen eyes scanned the tiny crack that

Jo Bell seemed to be speaking to. There was a brown blur as Buster dropped to the floor of the case.

"He's dead!" Edith gasped.

"Don't worry. That's just his way . . . his way of arriving."

"Like a corpse!" Felix said.

"He's so flat. He doesn't even look like a spider," Julep said. "More like a paint chip."

"Well, I am a spider." A voice came from the little fleck of brown, amazing the family, except for Jo Bell, even more. Then, one at a time, Buster's eight legs appeared and he staggered to his feet. "I am a spider, but nothing compared to you, of course. I'm not really toxic. I can only raise the occasional welt on a human."

"Please, dear," Edith interjected. "We don't talk about such things."

"Oh, I'm sorry. But Felix is right, too. My weaving skills are quite modest. The marbled orb weavers and the strawberry orb weavers can do pyramids and cylindrical orbs. They're quite fantastic."

"Quit apologizing for what you're not!" Jo Bell roared.

"Oh, sorry!" Buster said.

Edith stepped up to the walnut orb weaver.

"Now, Buster, I've organized night patrols against those revolting silverfish."

"Don't call them revolting if you expect me to eat them, Mom," Julep whined.

"Point taken, Julep. The silverfish are not revolting, but whining is."

"Touché!" Felix whispered.

SIX
Night Patrol

"Forward, march!" Felix barked.

Jo Bell shuddered with embarrassment.

"I will do a short recon mission to assess the enemy position. When I report back to Mom, I'll deploy troops. That's you."

"Oh, Felix dear, what would I do without you!" Edith cried.

Gimme a break, Jo Bell thought, but she kept quiet.

"Well, military history *is* more useful than fashion history."

That did it. Jo Bell could no longer remain quiet. "Felix, I could just bite off that fresh new leg of yours! You're such a know-it-all!"

"Now, now, children. No squabbling. Felix, we'll wait here for your report."

"I think that was snotty of Felix, Jo Bell. I really do," Julep offered.

"Thanks," Jo Bell muttered. "Well, let's just wait until the supreme commander of our allied forces returns." She sighed.

"What's with the fresh new leg for your brother?" Buster asked.

"Here's the short answer: Felix used to be passionate about music. Wanted to be a conductor. Then he got his leg whacked off by Leon Brinsky, conductor of a philharmonic in Los Angeles. End of story."

"Is that why your mom is so protective of Felix? She makes a big fuss over him."

"You noticed?" Jo Bell was stunned. This was some spider! He was sensitive, even though he seemed so obsessed with venom — their venom.

"Yeah. She can't take her eyes off Felix's webs."

"You saw that?"

"Yes, hope you're not mad."

"No, no, not at all. I'm glad someone was paying attention to me."

"Anytime." Buster paused. "Listen, I have a question."

"Sure."

"Felix didn't actually bite that conductor, did he?"

"Of course not." Jo Bell cocked her head and studied Buster with her six eyes. "You don't get it, do you?"

"Get what?"

"About us — brown recluses, *Loxosceles reclusa*. You see, we don't have to bite humans to scare the daylights out of them. Our reputation does it. One look at Felix peeping over that music stand, and Leon Brinsky panicked. Slashed down with his baton, then promptly fainted."

"Wow!" Buster was clearly impressed.

"It's not a wow situation, Buster. It means we

spend our lives on the run. First word of a brown recluse on the premises, the E-Men show up with silver tanks of poisonous gas."

"That's what happened?"

"Time and time again. That's why we wound up here. And we hope to stay — at least for a while."

At that moment, Felix returned.

"Attention!" he barked.

"Gather round, children." Edith waved five of her legs to motion them over. "Let's listen now to Felix's report. He does this so well!" Edith beamed at her only son.

"As you know, John Adams's personal library is kept on the balcony over there — just opposite our web. The Adams collection is very vulnerable. I heard Tom talking about it on the phone this morning. Since it's up on the balcony" — Felix waved his new leg to indicate the balcony — "it requires a climb of three meters."

"Do we have to use the metric system?" Julep complained. "I haven't learned that yet."

"All right, almost ten feet," Felix snapped. "A big group of silverfish — and a few glue bugs — have moved from the southwest corner of the balcony to the northwest corner. Henceforth, I'll refer to this as the geography section because that's where the Adams atlas is kept."

"No! Not John Adams's personal atlas!" Edith sighed. "Children, as you know, John Adams was the second president of the United States. His books are especially valuable because he scribbled little notes in them."

"I thought we weren't supposed to scribble in books," Julep said.

"If you're the president of the United States, you can scribble on anything you want," Jo Bell said.

"But proceed, dear." Edith nodded at Felix. "Explain your strategy."

Jo Bell couldn't bear how her mother fawned over Felix. And the more her mother did, the more insufferable he became.

"The southern flank of this quadrant is vulnerable. I would suggest after our initial climb a sneak attack. We'll gather at Checkpoint Quincy to begin our climb. You all know where that is — just over the doorway."

Jo Bell yawned.

"Are you bored, Jo Bell?" Felix asked. "I suggest you listen up!"

"Oh, no, not bored, just curious."

"What about, dear?" her mother asked.

"I find it fascinating how one minute Felix is an artist, and the next some kind of military expert."

"They're both art forms," Felix replied rather snootily. "There is a design to a military campaign just as there is a design for a web. Now, if I may continue?"

"Yes, dear, please do," Edith said. "The silverfish must be stopped before it's too late."

Felix looked more smug than ever, and Jo Bell started to feel as if she needed two more eyes to take in all of his fat head.

"For our climb, use number two quality silk." Felix then turned to Buster. "In orb weavers, I believe our number two is your number five. Strong, highly flexible, with a good amount of stretch, but it doesn't go all loopy on you."

"Yes, I believe you're right," Buster said.

"I have extensive knowledge of orb weaver silk — some remarkable grades, if I do say so," Felix continued.

Jo Bell thought she would vomit.

"He's unbearable!" she whispered to Julep, who was playing with a dead glue bug she had found.

"I can't believe I'm passing up this glue bug, but I can't eat another bite."

"Don't worry," Felix said. "We'll haul them back in my newly designed web, which is not only elegant but has amazing hauling abilities. We'll break into teams. Mom, you and Julep are one team. Jo Bell, you take Buster. I'll roam

and supervise all of you. Assault Team One."
He nodded at Edith and Julep. "You should
head directly for the atlas. Jo Bell, you and
Buster need to go to call number 915.4. It's
one of the few prints left of a sketch that Paul
Revere did of the Boston Massacre. The sketch
is now being attacked. It's massacre twice over,
first by the British soldiers and now by the
silverfish."

"May I say something?" Buster asked in
almost a whisper.

"Yes, but be quick about it," Felix snapped.

All twenty-four eyes were now riveted on
Buster.

"I have been here for a while and I am
familiar with the Adams collection. There is
something terribly important I need to tell you."

"What's that?" Jo Bell asked.

"There's a drawing in there of Crispus
Attucks, the first African American to die in the
Revolution. To die once is bad enough, but to

die again when the silverfish eat him is unthink-able." A new somberness seemed to envelop the four spiders.

"What do you mean?" Felix whispered.

"If the silverfish eat the drawing of Crispus, he will be gone. Gone from all memory if there isn't another drawing of him. He sacrificed his life for this country, and the silverfish are devouring the evidence!"

"We'll save him," Jo Bell said. "Buster, you and I can save him together."

"Perhaps I should go with you," Felix said. "This is a very urgent mission."

"No, Felix," Edith said. "Jo Bell and Buster can handle this. Let's stick to your original strategy."

Jo Bell's six eyes were shining as she looked at her mom. *Finally!* she thought. *Finally, it's not all about Felix.*

"All right," Felix barked. "Now prepare to climb!"

*   *   *

At precisely one minute after seven o'clock, according to the clock on the wall, the five spiders' spinnerets began to contract. Seconds later, they were squeezing liquid silk from their spigots for hoist lines. Attaching their lines to Checkpoint Quincy, they began to climb a vertical silken highway. On glimmering threads they swung through the amber light of the rare books foyer. They traveled steadily upward with singularly graceful motions to the lofty heights of the John Adams collection balcony shelves.

Forty minutes later, Felix had reached the recessed lighting fixtures just above the balcony. When the rest of the spiders arrived, he gave a silent signal with his two forelegs, or pedipalps, to indicate a steady stream of silverfish flowing like a trickling creek toward the atlas.

"Shocking! Positively shocking," Edith gasped.

Felix waved his pedipalps wildly for silence.

"No talking!" Of course, spiders do not exactly talk but, instead, communicate by sending out vibratory signals. The leg hairs of spiders contain some of the most highly refined sensors of any animal on earth.

An even larger infestation of silverfish awaited Jo Bell and Buster at their destination. The insects' long, flattish bodies seemed to be oozing in and out of the huge folio with the precious drawing of Crispus Attucks. "Thank God they don't have wings," Jo Bell muttered.

"I'll do a dead drop in from the top of the folio," Buster said.

"Be careful of the cracks. You might drop into the wrong place," Jo Bell warned. The leather cases and folios that held so many of the rare book treasures seemed more like mummies than books.

"Okay, I'll come in from the side," Buster said.

Jo Bell spotted the long antennae of several silverfish poking out from the edges of the folio.

Three seconds later, Jo Bell and Buster were inside the pages. The damage was impressive.

"Good grief, Buster. Look at poor Crispus! They are all over him."

"You go for the head, Jo Bell. The head's the most important thing. We can't have a hero without a face. I'll get the silverfish at his feet."

Jo Bell swung down on a bouncy thread of number four grade silk through the volley of silent gunfire on the page and knocked two silverfish senseless with a double injection of venom.

She rolled them to the edge of the engraving and returned to the fray, making her way toward the hero's face. From the corners of three of her eyes, she saw that Buster had arrived at Attucks's feet and was working feverishly to wrap up a silverfish and a glue bug, using his super-sticky binding silk. Within another two minutes, a dozen insect bodies were scattered across the engraving — from the cobblestones of King Street to the tippy-top of the state house.

"We saved him!" Jo Bell exclaimed.

Together they began to walk slowly around the image of the man who lay sprawled in the streets. They had rescued him from a second death. They had saved the memory of Crispus Attucks, the evidence that he died a true patriot for the cause of freedom.

SEVEN
Christmas in July

It was well after midnight when Edith, her children, and Buster returned to the display case. The night raid on the Adams collection had been their most successful yet.

"I'm in a webbish mood!" Edith declared. "Yes, it's time for a new web. We need one to store all the silverfish we've hauled back. Anyone want to help?"

"Your mother certainly is energetic!" Buster whispered.

"I know, and just hours ago she was complaining about old age. But she likes to show off our catch to Tom. That's why she picked this display case. Hardly anyone ever comes by it. And since we've been here, Tom has put it on the No Dust list. He sometimes tidies it up, but he's always sure not to wipe out our webs."

By now, Edith was skibbling around the case. "I think we'll have the main socializing web in this corner. But next to it, I'll weave a storage web for the silverfish. We can just dip in as the mood strikes us." She paused. "You have to admit that despite how loathsome these pests are, they are rather pretty — they seem to glint in the light. Why . . . why . . ." Edith's voice filled with excitement. "It's almost like Christmas!"

"Christmas in July!" came a voice from the floor.

"Fatty!" the Deadlies exclaimed in unison.

"Fatty, darling Fatty! What brings you here?" Edith asked.

"I could not take another second of that infernal flamenco," said the big cat with a delicate shudder. "The constant thumping! Dancing,

they call it! I call it clodhopping. Have you ever heard of a cat with a headache?"

"No, dear, I haven't," Edith said.

"Well, I have one! So I thought I'd take a break and come here for a few days. And it seems it is also Christmas? What was that you were saying, Edith?"

"Oh, just a funny little memory of mine."

"Webtime story! Mom, a webtime story, please!" Julep jumped up and down on all eight legs. "Please! Please! Puleeze!"

"Well, for silk's sake, let me finish this web first!"

"Can we hear the one about the Place Where Time Has Stopped?"

"Oh, Julep, you always ask for that one," Jo Bell groaned.

"But we all love the story, Jo Bell. You know we do."

It was true. Despite Jo Bell's groaning, it was their favorite. Jo Bell's only hesitation was that, although the story never wore thin, the dream of finding a wonderful place where spiders could live with no fear of E-Men seemed as far away as ever. The Boston Public Library was the closest the family had ever come to the Place Where Time Has Stopped, where they believed humans and spiders lived together with no fear.

The Smoots were the only dark cloud in this splendid library, and Edith still didn't know about them.

Buster had never heard any webtime stories. He was intrigued by the idea of a Place Where Time Has Stopped.

But now Felix was echoing Jo Bell. "A new story, Mom!"

"All right! All right! Just let me finish here," Edith said.

A few minutes later, the dim golden dusk of the display case was spangled by the silverfish that Edith and her children had woven into the storage web.

"It reminds me of one Christmas in particular," Edith marveled. "It's like tinsel on a Christmas tree!"

"Which Christmas, Mom?" Julep said. "Come on, tell us."

"Oh, it was so long ago. I hardly remember all the details. I think I was even younger than you, Julep."

Julep peered at her mother. It was unimaginable that her mother had ever been that young. Had she ever whined — as everyone was always accusing Julep of doing?

"Well, children, once upon a time so long ago, when I was but a wee thing . . ."

There was nothing quite like Edith's webtime story voice. Jo Bell could tell that Buster was instantly enchanted. His chelicerae, his spider jaws, dropped wide open. He had read and read and read his entire life, but he had never really heard a story told. Buster had never felt ashamed or sorry for being what he would describe as an "instant orphan." In fact, Buster had thought that his biggest problem in life was not being venomous. But now he realized he was wrong. He was lonely. And he always had been lonely.

As he perched in a corner of the somewhat messy web, enveloped by the bluish light — for brown recluse silk has a tinge of blue — he felt as if he had finally arrived in a snug harbor. A silken harbor where the threads were stirred by a soft voice.

He knew about *The Nutcracker*. A score by Tchaikovsky was in the music manuscript room, and he had read the story of the ballet that began on Christmas Eve, when a little girl was given the gift of a doll — a nutcracker prince. That night she dreams that the prince enters a fierce battle with a mouse king. But never had the magic of the story seemed more real than now.

"It was in the first theater I ever visited. It was called the Palace, in the great city of Chicago. I can't remember where we had come from, or exactly where we went after the E-Men arrived. It was all such a blur. But I do remember my dear dad and mum and your great-aunt Tessie had decided we should weave our webs in the tippy-top of the Christmas tree. It was an artificial tree, of course, and it rose out of the stage in the first act. When the ballet starts, the scene is set for a lovely party to begin at the Stahlbaum house. It is a grand house, for the Stahlbaums are very rich, and every Christmas Eve, they give a wonderful party. Clara and Fritz are their children."

"How old are they?" Jo Bell interrupted.

"Oh, I would say just about your age and Felix's age — middle grade and elementary school." This was an influence from the time Edith had spent at the Martin Luther King Jr. Elementary School in Phoenix, Arizona. It had left a lasting impression, and she often thought of her children in terms of grade levels. Felix was a solid sixth grader, Jo Bell a seventh grader, and Julep a kindergartner. Or possibly a first grader.

"Isn't there anybody my age?" Julep whined.

"You mean pre-K?" Felix snorted.

"Children, stop that. No interruptions, please. All eyes on me!"

Buster was shaking with frustration at the interruptions.

"As I was saying, there is a party, and the children's godfather arrives." Edith gave a quick glance up toward Fatty, her own children's godspider, who had settled on the top of the display case. "He brings presents for Clara and Fritz. To Clara he gives a doll — a nutcracker prince. Fritz is jealous and a fight breaks out between the children, breaking the doll. But that's only the beginning of the story. For after the guests leave and the clock strikes midnight, strange things begin to happen. Clara starts to shrink, and the Christmas tree begins to grow and grow and grow. Oh, it was a wonderful feeling for all of us as the tree rose up, up, and up, as if on threads of silk. I can just see my mother and Aunt Tessie, their twelve eyes sparkling. It was as if we were at the very heart of a miracle. We could look out from our web and see the audience gasping in wonder. Children wiggling in their seats suddenly grew still, their eyes round with disbelief!"

"Too bad little human kids have just two eyes," Julep moaned softly. "There's so much to see!"

By this time, twenty-six spider eyes were round with disbelief. Edith's silken voice wove through the night as the silverfish glimmered in the gossamer lattice of threads. Edith was not only a spinner of webs, but a spinner of enchantment.

EIGHT
To Catch a Thief

Jo Bell nestled in the taffeta petals of a rose pinned to the brim of the elderly lady's hat in the Bates reading room of the Boston Public Library. Buster had never bothered to find out the lady's name. He simply called her The Hat. The lady was reading a book entitled *Elements of Crime Detection* by Ellis Frumkin. And Jo Bell was reading alongside her.

A footprint is a treasure trove of information. A detective can not only determine the type of shoe worn but can also reveal the height and weight of the suspect, where he or she has been, and where he or she might be going. Recall if you will the Sherlock Holmes story "A Scandal in

Bohemia" and Holmes's brilliant detection of where his partner Watson has just been: "It is simplicity itself. . . . My eyes tell me that on the inside of your left shoe, just where the firelight strikes it, the leather is scored by six almost parallel cuts. Obviously they have been caused by someone who has very carelessly scraped round the edges of the sole in order to remove crusted mud from it.

But, thought Jo Bell, *we don't have to deduce anything to know who committed the crime. It was Agnes Smoot!* She had learned a lot about fingerprints, witness protection, and dragnets set up to catch criminals. But none of it helped.

Jo Bell made a decision. She crawled out of the taffeta rose, then cast a dragline to lower herself down. The Hat seemed to sense something out of the corner of her eye and raised a hand with liver-colored age spots to flick Jo Bell away.

Don't do it, lady!

It was a narrow escape. Jo Bell's spinnerets went into high gear and she squeezed out a half foot more of line to The Hat's shoulder. Next she skibbled down a sleeve, hopped from there to the desk, and cast another dragline to swing herself under the long tables of the reading room.

Buster had camped out on the collar of a man who had fallen asleep reading old issues of the *Boston Globe*.

"What's up, Jo Bell — want to read this? The most fascinating art crime ever was right here in Boston. The thieves tied up two security guards with duct tape and made off with three hundred million dollars' worth of art. The crime was never solved."

"That's just the problem, Buster," Jo Bell said.

"What do you mean?"

"Our crime is solved! We know who did it. It's Agnes Smoot and her husband!"

"I still don't understand what you're saying."

For someone as smart as Buster, he could be a bit dense at times, Jo Bell thought.

"Look, we've spent all morning reading about crime detection. But we've already detected the crime. What we have to figure out is how to catch the thieves!"

"It would be so much easier with venom," Buster said mournfully.

"Buster, you are venom obsessed!" Jo Bell shouted. "Get over it. Venom is out of the question." She immediately felt terrible. She shouldn't have yelled at him. Buster was so sweet, and even kind of cute in his own way. She didn't want to hurt his feelings. But he did have a venom fixation. In a softer voice she continued, "We need to read about catching a thief — entrapment."

"Entrapment! Of course you're right, Jo Bell! The real problem is that Tom doesn't know what's happening and there's no way we can tell him. I mean, he doesn't speak spider and we don't speak human. It's really amazing that your friend Fat Cat can understand us."

"He has since birth," Jo Bell replied.

"Since he was born? Astounding."

"Oh, no — not Fatty's birth. Ours. When Mom arrived at the philharmonic hall, she was on the brink of spinning an egg sac. She couldn't find a safe place to put it, but Fatty seemed so friendly that she used signs to ask him if she could stick it in his ear. And 'Voilà!' as Fatty would say. The rest is history."

"So the first time Fatty heard spider talk was from the three of you?"

"Yep — squabbling, arguing for the best space in his ear when we hatched out. His ear is very nice. So soft and furry. And he heard Mom sing us lullabies. He was speaking spider in no time."

"You don't say!"

"Yes. Communication with Fatty is easy. But with Tom it's another story."

"And that is our problem."

"Tom never goes to the fashion portfolios, so how will he ever discover what's missing?"

"And he doesn't go to the map collection, either. Now, if it were something to do with, say, Egypt, he'd be on those two crooks like — pardon the expression—like a spider on a glue bug."

NINE
Eldridge Montague Strikes Again

"Where did everyone go?" Jo Bell asked when she returned to the display case.

"I'm here," Edith said.

"But where's Fatty? Julep? Felix?"

"Well, let's see. Fatty went down to the library café to see if there's any garbage about. He loves those tuna wraps they sell. Felix is hanging around in the military section. There's a Civil War book that caught his fancy. I myself was just about to skibble over to an adorable miniature Book of Common Prayer."

Borrring! Jo Bell thought, but didn't say it out loud.

"Julep most likely is back at the circus—the pop-up book. She loves swinging on that paper trapeze."

"Wrong!" Julep sang out as she lithely made her way down through the silverfish in the storage web. "Not in the circus book—the toilet pop-up book."

"The toilet book!" Edith and Jo Bell both exclaimed.

"Not what you think. Not that kind of toilet, but twa-let! Jo Bell, you should know. It's the French word for dressing. It doesn't mean pooping. It's all the little bottles and hairbrushes and stuff that human ladies keep on their dressing tables. It's so much fun. I'd love to try on makeup. Mascara—six eyes but no eyelashes! What a waste!"

"Well, dear, I'm glad that you're diversifying your interests and not limiting yourself to the circus."

"And after lunch, I'm going back to slip into

an Egyptian pop-up — a book on the pyramids! Just imagine, Mom, mummies!" Julep laughed gleefully. "Get it, Mom — mummies?"

"Yes, dear, a pun."

"But I'm starving!" Julep said.

"Well, eat up some of those silverfish," Edith replied. "You know they don't keep forever, and they taste so much better when they're fresh. All their innards dry up over time and they become much less nutritious."

All this talk about food got Jo Bell hungry as well. "I'll join you."

The two sisters went to the storage web and shook down a silverfish. It was much easier eating them on the floor of the display cabinet than midair in the web.

Jo Bell and Julep made themselves comfortable on either side of the creature. "Okay, I found the original puncture wounds," Julep said.

Jo Bell was impressed. Julep had really matured since they had arrived at the library. Before, she would have charged in and made new fang holes, which often resulted in wasted food. The two sisters emitted a small amount of digestive fluids into the silverfish carcass so the bug's guts would liquefy and could be sucked out.

"I'm feeling a tad peckish myself," Edith said. "Mind if I take a sip?"

"Sure, Mom," both daughters replied.

Edith began to drink, then looked up after her first swallow. "Lacks character. It's not very robust in flavor."

"Not as robust as a cockroach," Jo Bell replied.

As Jo Bell slurped up the silverfish gut juice, she thought about the problem she and Buster were facing. Sometimes she thought she should tell her mother about it, or maybe Fatty. But there was something deep within her that wanted to figure it out herself — well, with Buster, of course. What a triumph that would be!

"You're being awfully quiet, dear," Edith said to her elder daughter.

"Just thinking."

"Thinking about Buster, I bet," Julep said, and giggled. "You've got a crush on Buster!"

"Oh, shut up!"

"Girls! I hate that kind of bickering," Edith said, glaring at her daughters.

Jo Bell retreated once more into silence.

When Jo Bell woke up, her mother was bustling about, stringing up a cockroach that looked as polished as the floors.

"A cockroach!" Jo Bell exclaimed.

"Yes, I thought it would be a break from the silverfish." The cockroach's glistening ebony carapace made Jo Bell's mouth water.

"Where did you find it?"

"In *Uncle Tom's Cabin*."

Jo Bell was slightly confused. "Tom has a cabin here? I thought he had an apartment on Berkeley Street."

"Not that Tom, dear. I am talking about the book *Uncle Tom's Cabin*."

"I've never heard of it!" Felix, who had just arrived, said rather dismissively.

"You of all spiders should have heard of it, dear boy," said Edith. "You've been studying all those maps of the Civil War."

"Yes, and one is missing! It looks as if it has been cut right out of the book."

Jo Bell felt her spinnerets contract. So Eldridge Montague, Agnes Smoot's husband, had struck again. Should she tell the rest of her family what she knew, what she had seen? But if she did, Felix would take over the whole plan. Felix was the bossiest spider ever.

She had to report the new theft to Buster as soon as possible. But not before feasting on the cockroach. It seemed like forever since she had sucked up the sweet juices of a cockroach.

"So who's this Uncle Tom?" Felix asked.

"It's a book," Edith repeated. "When Abraham Lincoln met the author, Harriet Beecher Stowe, he said, 'So this is the little lady who made this big war.' He was talking about the Civil War."

"A lady started one of the most important wars in American history!" Felix was flabbergasted.

"Don't underestimate us," Jo Bell muttered.

"How did she start it? Did she fire a cannon? Assassinate someone?" Felix asked.

"No, dear, she wrote a book about slavery. Uncle Tom was a slave, a pious man who kept his faith despite the horrendous treatment he suffered at the hands of his owner. And this darned cockroach was about to chomp one of the most important passages. But" — Edith's six eyes glittered — "I got that roach with my port fang just in time. One of the most important books in American literature has been saved!" Edith took a triumphant slurp out of the offending cockroach.

A few minutes later, Jo Bell crawled up the side of the case, looking for Buster, who could most often be found either in the Edgar Allan Poe collection or around the corner where the Sherlock Holmes papers were kept.

She found Buster in a folio of articles by Poe for a magazine called *Alexander's Weekly Messenger.*

"Oh, hi, Jo Bell. Hey, I got a riddle for you."

"But I have something to tell you."

"Wait just a second. This is so clever." When Buster got an idea, there was little chance of distracting him.

"What's the difference between herb soup and turtle soup?"

"What?" Jo Bell asked, trying to muster some enthusiasm for something that sounded as bad as any of Julep's knock-knock jokes.

"One is herb soup and the other is soup herb."

"I don't get it."

"Superb! The soup is superb!"

"Oh," said Jo Bell. "Listen, Buster, I have something serious to say."

"I'm all ears," Buster said, then started giggling again. "There's a good one about ears, too."

"Spare me. Now get this! Felix just reported that a map was cut out from a book about the Battle of Antietam."

Buster grew still. "What! That was the single most important battle of the Civil War! Eldridge is obviously getting bolder, and so is Agnes. We have to stop them!"

"We have to make Tom realize what is happening. If he only spoke spider!" Jo Bell sighed. And even though she was still standing on all of her eight legs, her whole body seemed to slump.

TEN
Forget Spider Speak!

Two days later, the library reopened after a long holiday weekend. As was Tom's habit since the Deadlies had arrived in the Rare Books Department, he came over to the display case to greet them and check up on their catch.

"I hope you enjoyed the Fourth of July, kids!" Tom said, leaning over the display case. "Oh! My goodness, you had a busy weekend. Look at those silverfish."

If only he spoke spider, Jo Bell thought for the hundredth time.

"And goodness, that web looks rather festive with all those silvery critters dangling."

Tom understands so much. What other human

being would appreciate us the way Tom does! Jo Beth thought. It was all very frustrating.

The phone at the main desk began to ring, and Tom walked away to answer it.

"Yes, this is Tom Parker, conservator of rare books. Indeed we do have the *Wurmach Encyclopedia of Hieroglyphs*. . . . Yes. . . . It's one of three existing first editions from 1825. As you know, Wurmach was a cryptologist — an expert in code breaking."

Codes! Cryptology! Egyptians! Hieroglyphs! Of course! thought Jo Bell. *That's how we have to do it!*

Tom turned to his assistant, Rosemary. "Tomorrow someone's coming in early for the *Wurmach Encyclopedia*. It's call number 932.W4."

"Right-o, Tom," Rosemary answered.

Jo Bell skittled over to Buster's favorite bookshelf in the Rare Books Department.

"BUSTER!" she screeched.

"Whoa! Are you trying to start an earthquake here?" Buster said.

"Listen, Buster, I just had a brainstorm. Guess how we can get Tom's attention."

"How?" He crawled out of the folio.

"Forget spider speak." Jo Bell waved four of her legs wildly about in all directions. "We need to write him a message. One that only Tom can understand. Not Smoot or Montague. Don't you see the answer, Buster?"

"What? What are you saying?"

"Codes, cryptology, and Tom's favorite — hieroglyphics!"

Buster staggered slightly. "Jo Bell, you're a genius!" He paused, then added in a rather tentative voice, "But how do we do it? How do we write the code?"

"In silk and silverfish. Think of it as a kind of dragnet — because it is, in a sense."

"Yes, of course!"

She told him how Tom had admired the silverfish strung up in the family web. "He said it was festive, Buster. I mean he really appreciated the design."

"But we don't know hieroglyphics."

"We can learn enough. Julep has been hanging out in that pop-up pyramid book for the last three days. We'll ask her."

"But you didn't want to tell your family."

"The time has come," Jo Bell answered solemnly. "We need all the help we can get."

The nineteenth-century pop-up books were on a mezzanine of the Rare Books Department of the library. The quickest way to get to them was through air-conditioning vents. So Jo Bell and Buster let themselves get sucked up in a cool draft.

"I'm not sure where the pop-up books are, actually," Jo Bell said.

"I know. You have to go past the sacred texts, then take a left."

"Sacred texts — we might run into Mom. She's got a thing about prayer books."

When they arrived a few minutes later, Jo Bell exclaimed, "Good grief! There are a lot of pop-up books."

"Wouldn't Julep be in one that is already

opened on the reading tables? I mean, what's the sense of messing about in a folded-up pop-up book?" Buster said.

"True." They made their way to the reading tables at the end of the fourth row of stacks.

"My goodness, it's like a miniature world here, isn't it?" Jo Bell wondered aloud as she looked at the books spread out on a large table. The first thing she noticed were the red and white stripes of the three-ring circus tent. In the center ring were paper animals, elephants whose trunks could wag and tigers who prowled. The second ring had half a dozen clowns, one riding a pony. Another could be made to jump through a hoop. The third ring was Julep's favorite, for this ring belonged to the aerial artists. Tiny little paper people swung on trapezes no thicker than splinters and pranced on tightropes made of thread. It was here that they spied Julep swinging out among the frozen paper figures.

"What are you doing here?" Jo Bell called. "I thought you were in Egypt — the pyramids."

"I was. I just came over for a break. But why are you here?" Julep asked.

"It's a long story," Jo Bell replied.

"A sad story," Buster added.

"Is Mom okay?" Julep blurted out. "Did she get squished or —" Julep began to tremble.

"Mom's fine! It's nothing like that." Jo Bell felt terrible. Suddenly, Julep seemed so tiny and defenseless. "Oh, Julep, I didn't mean to worry you!"

"Well, what's so sad?" Julep asked with visible relief.

"Someone is cutting pages out of books, stealing maps. There are crooks in the library."

"What?" Julep gasped.

And so Jo Bell and Buster told the story of Agnes Smoot and Eldridge Montague.

"It seems," Julep said slowly when they had finished, "that the problem is getting Tom's attention. Finding a way to tell him since he doesn't speak spider."

"Exactly," Jo Bell replied. "But he does speak hieroglyphics."

"No one speaks hieroglyphics," Julep corrected. "It's a language for writing only. Writing in pictures."

"Do you know how to write it?" Buster asked.

"Uh, well, just my name and a few other letters, that's all," Julep replied.

"Can you show us?" Buster asked.

"Sure!" Julep suddenly seemed to grow to twice her size. No one ever asked her opinion about anything. Most of the time, her older brother and sister reminded her how babyish she was. This was definitely a non-pre-K moment, and Julep intended to make the most of it.

She immediately cast another dragline to the tightrope and began her ascent. Then, in the dim shadows of the big tent, Julep began her own aerial ballet. She embroidered the air with silken shapes of birds and snakes, reeds and crouching lions.

"That's your name?" Jo Bell's voice quivered with amazement.

"Yep, but I'm not done."

Julep continued her inscriptions, and five minutes later, another word appeared.

"Two words!" Buster exclaimed.

"What does it say?" Jo Bell asked.

Her little sister looked down at her and burst out with a vibration that shivered the silk threads under the big top and set the paper figures aflutter.

"JULEP RULES!"

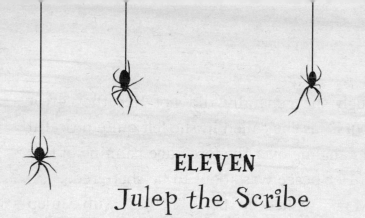

ELEVEN
Julep the Scribe

Jo Bell glanced at the remaining silverfish twirling slightly in the still air of the display case. Edith had just finished an addition to their regular web that extended from the southeast corner of the case to the southwest corner, where one of the most beautiful books in the entire library rested on a velvet cloth. The book, a tenth-century volume from China, was set in a fantastically crafted metal box. On the edges of the book's pages was a painting that only became visible when the book was shut. The painting depicted a winter landscape of billowing, snow-covered mountains. This type of book art was called fore-edge painting, and the delicacy of the work was remarkable. Edith claimed that although she generally did not like the "great outdoors," as she called it, she felt quite peaceful when dangling over the fore-edge painting of this book. Her peace was about to be shattered.

"Mom," called Jo Bell. "Felix . . . uh, Julep and Buster and I have something to tell you."

Edith inhaled sharply. "Oh, no! You haven't been seen. Please don't tell me that. My poor heart can't take it." The anguish in Edith's voice was so strong, one could almost touch it.

"No, Mom, we haven't been seen."

In Edith's mind, there was absolutely nothing worse than being discovered by humans — humans other than Tom Parker. Edith had spent her youth on the run, fleeing E-Men with their gleaming silver tanks of poison attached to snakey fumigation hoses. When she became a mother herself, she vowed this wandering would cease. The worst thing in Edith's mind was to be unsettled.

"Edith?" Fatty called.

"Oh, Fatty, you've come back again!"

"I missed all of you so much."

"Well, I'm afraid you've come when . . ." Edith's voice dwindled away.

"Oh, dear!" Fatty said. "What's the problem?"

"We don't quite know yet. Jo Bell, will you continue?"

Jo Bell took a deep breath. "I witnessed something pretty awful a few days back. A person tearing a page from the fashion portfolio."

"What?!?" Edith gasped.

"Yes, Mom, Agnes Smoot. And that's not all. Her husband, Eldridge Montague, has been stealing maps out of old books for years. We have to stop them somehow."

"Why didn't you tell us sooner? We could have helped," Edith said.

"Well," Jo Bell's voice cracked a bit. She wobbled on at least three of her eight legs.

"What is it, dear?"

She began again. "I wanted to do this all by myself. Well, I mean with Buster's help, but we needed to figure out a plan. These criminals have gone undetected for a long time. No one ever really checks out those old map books or the fashion portfolios. So the problem is how to draw Tom's attention to the crime."

"And do you have a solution?" Felix asked. There was a hint of huffiness in his voice.

"We're going to leave Tom a message."

"Just how are you going to do that?" Felix asked with a sneer.

"Felix!" Edith said sharply. "I don't like that tone. Let Jo Bell explain."

"I think it would be best if I let Julep do the explaining," Jo Bell said, standing aside to give Julep the floor.

"Julep!" Edith, Felix, and Fat Cat all exclaimed at once.

"Yes! Me! Yours truly here. While Felix has been studying military history, and Mom has been crawling through old Bibles, I have spent quite a bit of time in the Egyptian pop-up books. I picked up a bit of hieroglyphics along the way."

"You understand hieroglyphics?" Fatty marveled.

"A bit, and I'm learning more every day. And Jo Bell says that I am to teach all of you," Julep said, with a pointed look at her bossy brother.

"We have to learn hieroglyphics to do this?" Felix said.

"Don't worry," Jo Bell replied. "Not that much. The message should be short and simple. But we don't have any time to lose."

Jo Bell turned to her mother. "This morning, Tom saw the silverfish threaded through our storage web. And do you know what he said, Mom?"

"No, dear. What?"

"He said, 'rather festive'!"

"Really?" Edith said with wonder.

"Quite remarkable," Fatty added. "A human being so attuned to something like that."

"It got us thinking that the silverfish are the perfect shape for making some of the letters," Julep said.

"Julep, show everyone how you can write your name," Jo Bell suggested.

Julep bounced up and down with excitement. She cast a dragline, swung up on it, and then dropped another almost parallel. As she spun and swung the silk, she whispered to herself, "Ascend, spin off, rappel, loop . . . easy on the descent, tie off."

Lovely shapes began to form in the air above the family. "Atta girl!" Buster called.

"What does it say, dear?" Edith asked when Julep was finished.

"Mom," Julep said softly.

TWELVE
Mom Meets Mummy

Pull that tab on that book, Fatty, and see what happens," Julep instructed.

The five spiders and Fat Cat had made their way to the pop-up books on the third floor.

"What is it?" Fatty asked.

"I was here the other day when a scholar was fiddling with this book, and I nearly fell off my dragline when I saw what happened."

Fatty pulled the tab and, suddenly, dozens of little paper Egyptians popped up.

"It's a funeral procession to the pyramid. See, they're putting the coffin — or sarcophagus — on a barge."

"My, my, Julep, I'm impressed. You've

learned a lot in here." Edith was beaming with delight.

"Want to go inside the Beautiful House?" Julep asked. "There are a lot of hieroglyphs in there and we could begin our lessons."

"What do they do in the Beautiful House?"

"Make the mummies."

"How?" Felix asked.

"I'll wait outside." Fatty had no choice, but he was happy not to be with the group when he heard Julep's little voice explaining the procedure.

"It's very complicated to get a dead person ready for eternal life. First they have to take out all the stuff like the liver." Julep turned to her mother. "Mom, do we have livers?"

"I . . . I'm not sure, dear."

"Anyway," Julep continued, "they cut all that stuff out and they even weigh the heart. If it's light, it means you've led a good life. If not, you've been bad — weight of sin, you know. Weighs a lot."

"I bet Agnes Smoot's and Eldridge Montague's hearts put together don't weigh as much as a flea," Buster said.

Julep had hopped up onto a shelf that held a tiny paper jar with some hieroglyphs on it. "Your first word."

She tapped lightly on the series of five figures.

"So what does that spell in hieroglyphs?" Jo Bell asked.

"Brain. It's the jar they keep the brain in."

"Eeeew!" the four spiders and Fatty all said at once.

Julep continued, "The best part is how they get the brain out. You won't believe this." Julep was

bouncing around with great excitement now. "They liquefy it! They take the brain out with little hooks through the dead person's nose."

"Absolutely revolting," Fatty said.

Julep had begun swinging on a dragline from one jar to the next. "This one here is for the lungs."

"Ick!"

"This one is for the guts."

"Yuck!"

"Why did they save all this disgusting stuff?" Jo Bell asked.

"The dead person needs to have it for his next life. They believed that."

"I'm not sure what good a liquefied brain is

going to do you in the hereafter, and I certainly don't see why knowing how to write words like 'lung' and 'guts' is going to help us tip off Tom about these criminals," Felix muttered.

"Mommy," Julep wailed. "He's making fun of me."

"I think," Buster began, "Julep is teaching us the alphabet so we can write whatever words we want in hieroglyphics. No one will know their meaning except Tom."

"Yes," Julep said with a grateful glance at Buster. "We should go to the pyramid. There are a lot more hieroglyphs in there."

It felt to Jo Bell as if dark shadows were reaching out to grab them as they entered the pyramid. The little group followed Julep down some stairs.

"Please look left," Julep said in the voice of an experienced tour guide. "You will notice quite a bit of writing on the walls. We are now in the burial chamber. Let's be respectful as we approach the sarcophagus of the lady. She's a princess, Princess Henttawi. It's open so we can see the mummy."

The five spiders crept forward. Julep turned to Edith. "Mom, meet mummy."

"The wrapping technique is rather similar to ours," Edith commented. "She could be a June bug all wrapped up like that."

There was writing all over the place — on the sarcophagus, the walls, and the boat that was supposed to transport the dead person to the next world. Most important, there was a papyrus scroll called the Book of the Dead tucked at the feet of the mummy.

The five spiders visited the pyramid three times in all, and by the end of the third visit, they had learned enough hieroglyphs to write just about any word they wanted.

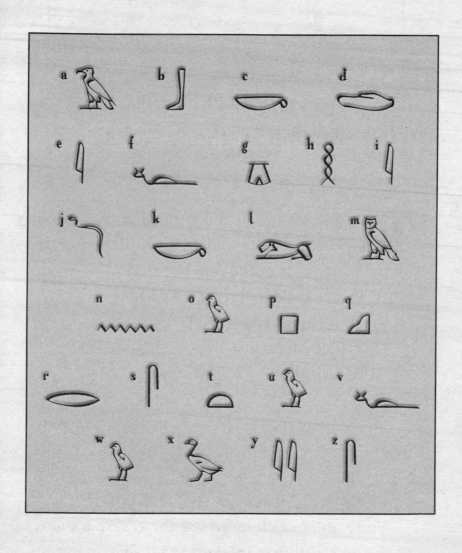

THIRTEEN
Blades in the Stacks

The spiders had left the pop-up book section and were stepping out of a ventilation grate on the main floor of the rare books reading room when Buster called, "Freeze! It's him!"

"Who?" Edith whispered.

"Eldridge Montague!"

"The map thief?" Jo Bell asked.

"Yes."

"Here you are, Professor Montague, the *New World Explorers' Atlas*," said Rosemary, handing Montague a valuable book.

"I knew it! I just knew it!" Buster screeched.

Edith and her children felt the reverberations of Buster's outburst in every nano-hair on their thirty-two legs.

"I knew it was only a matter of time until he decided to get into the sixteenth-century maps. There are books with maps by explorers like Ponce de León. He's going in with his blade!"

Jo Bell felt a tremor deep in her spinnerets. She had seen the shadow of a blade just the week before. It was dreadful. She pulled up seven of

her legs tightly so that she was clinging to her dragline with only one.

"I want to see this creep!" Felix hissed. "Follow me!"

Five minutes later, they were all nestled in an empty light socket above the desk where Eldridge Montague sat. Rosemary, Tom's assistant, had returned to her desk to answer a telephone call. *How convenient!* Jo Bell thought, for the ringing telephone muffled the soft zip of Montague's blade.

"That's how he does it! He waits until there's noise to cover the cutting sound. And please note that huge raincoat he is wearing. On the inside, it's lined with big pockets for the map he cuts out," Jo Bell whispered to her dumbstruck family.

The map was lovely. The paper — the color of weak tea — showed a hand-drawn map by the famous French explorer Samuel de Champlain. The prettiest part was the wide Atlantic Ocean with full-rigged ships and delicate drawings of leaping fish. Great forests and mountain ranges were rendered with tiny strokes of a very fine pen. And quicker than a wink, Eldridge Montague had slipped the priceless map into his raincoat.

Edith gasped. "Felix!"

But it was too late. Jo Bell, Julep, and Buster all caught a glimpse of what Edith had just seen. Felix had dropped a dragline into Eldridge Montague's pocket and was being swiftly transported — along with the map — out of the rare books room.

"Toodle-oo!" Montague called out merrily to Rosemary at the desk. Then, poking his head into Tom's conservator's room, he waved jauntily. "See you soon, old boy."

"What are we going to do?" Julep cried. Fatty, of course, was nowhere to be seen. Hanging out in the deserted stacks was one thing, but a cat couldn't exactly waltz into the reading room during library hours.

Edith gave a little moan and passed out cold.

Jo Bell gently tweaked the nano-hairs on her mother's various legs. "Mom! Mom!"

Finally, Edith came to. And was she mad! "What did that harebrained son of mine think he was doing?"

"He's read too much military history, I guess, Mom. He wants to be a hero," Jo Bell offered.

"He should have read enough to know that heroes often die," Edith fumed. "We have to go back to the display case to regroup until Fatty shows up this evening after closing hours." She looked up at the clock on the wall. "Thank goodness we don't have too long to wait. Just another two hours."

But those two hours seemed like an eternity. And when Fatty had not shown up by five thirty, the family really began to worry.

FOURTEEN
Fatty-at-Large

Fat Cat had seen everything. He had looked down in horror from a ceiling grate as Felix leapt into the thief's pocket. His first thought was *What is that kid trying to do? Lose another leg?* Adolescence was a trying time, but Felix was going to get himself squashed trying to be a hero.

Fatty had to think fast. He skedaddled down a back stairs that led to the library's main entrance on Dartmouth Street. He spotted Montague almost immediately. His raincoat flared out behind him as he went down the library's main granite stairs and turned toward Boylston Street. The sidewalks were thronged with people, for the weather had cooled and it was the start of a lovely summer evening. Fatty followed Montague as he crossed

Boylston Street, then Newbury, and walked another block to Commonwealth Avenue.

The broad avenue was lined on either side with elegant brick town houses. In April it looked as if it were snowing pink magnolia blossoms, for each tiny yard had a magnolia tree. Now, however, it was summer and the street was shaded by the deep green of magnolia leaves. Fatty crossed Commonwealth. At the corner of Dartmouth and Marlborough streets, he turned left. This was another elegant block, but the houses were somewhat smaller. Montague walked halfway down the street and then up the steps to number 16, which he entered.

Fat Cat leapt onto the black iron railing that lined the steps. There were three doorbells. One said BENNETT, on the third floor. One said CARLISLE/MILTON, on the second floor, and for the first-floor apartment, there were the names MONTAGUE/ DE FUNK.

Easy peasy, Fatty thought.

Five minutes later, he squeezed into the building through bulkhead cellar doors directly below Montague's study. The crook was having a drink and apparently some cocktail weenies wrapped in puff pastry. Fatty drooled. He loved cocktail weenies, but he could not be distracted at a time like this. His godspiderling was in the pocket of a thief.

Fatty pressed himself as close as possible to a floor grate. "Felix," he whispered. And because this faithful and very intelligent cat spoke spider, there were no meows and not a word was heard.

"Fatty!"

"Young man, you have really done it now! Your mother is a wreck."

"I had to, Fatty. But how did you get here?"

"I saw the whole thing — what happened in the reading room."

"So you know it was bad. The guy's terrible!" Felix exclaimed.

"That's no excuse. You have recklessly endangered your life."

"I'm not in his pocket anymore."

"Where are you exactly?"

"In a champagne glass," Felix answered.

Just then, footsteps were heard.

"Oh, darling, let's not have just plain old wine. Let's have a glass of the bubbly! This is such an occasion! The New France map! How much do you think we can sell it for?" It was Agnes Smoot, and both Fatty and Felix heard the big slobbery smooch she gave her husband.

Holy silk, Felix thought as he heard the

champagne cork pop, then felt the glass he was in being lifted.

"Get out of there, Felix!" Fatty cried, accidently letting out a little screech.

"Darling, is that a cat yowling?"

"Sounds like it, doesn't it? I'll go check." Felix felt the flute he was in being set back down on a table. When he picked up the vibrations of Agnes's and Eldridge's footsteps on the carpet, he quickly cast a dragline and hoisted himself out of the glass.

"Must have been one of those vile alley cats sniffing around the garbage. But I don't see anything from here," said Eldridge. "Now, you were asking about how much we could get for the New France map. Minimum a million dollars. But who knows what the gent at the French Institute might give us. He might pay double, I think!"

"Oh, Eldridge! You're a genius! We're on our way!" Agnes Smoot sighed. Then there was another slurpy Smoot smooch.

"I'll tuck this away for now," Eldridge said.

Fat Cat pressed his ear to the grate. He heard Eldridge walk about ten steps, then heard the sound of a drawer opening. It was a file cabinet. He could tell by the metallic noise as the drawer was pulled out.

"Felix!" cried Fatty. "You listen to me. Get down here this minute and come back with me, or else I'll drag you out by your fresh new leg!"

Felix was down the grate in a flash.

"Climb in my ear," Fat Cat ordered. "We'll get back in a jiff."

"You have to admit, Fatty, I did pick up some invaluable information," Felix said as he settled into the dense fluffiness of Fatty's furry ear.

"Possibly, but at great risk!"

"What do you mean, possibly? Fatty, don't you get it? You could sneak into Montague's apartment and bring those maps back to the Rare Books Department."

Fat Cat stopped dead in his tracks. "Are you

nuts? First of all, that is breaking and entering. It's a crime."

"They won't send a cat to jail."

"No, but possibly to the pound. And never mind that! You think I could go trotting along the streets of Boston with a million-dollar map in my mouth?"

"Oh, I never thought of that."

Fatty heaved a deep sigh. "Of course you didn't. You are young and reckless and on occasion incredibly stupid." He paused, then muttered, "Youth is wasted on the young."

"What's that you just said?"

"Youth is wasted on the young — George Bernard Shaw the playwright said it first."

"I don't think it's really wasted on me, Fatty."

"If you get yourself smushed, it will be."

It was a hard statement to argue with, and Felix remained silent.

FIFTEEN
T for Tom

Somehow Edith had pulled herself together — for her children. It was the hardest thing she had ever had to do. She had to trust that Felix, reckless as he was, would come back alive and with all eight legs attached! In the meantime, there was work to be done.

"Children," she said, turning to Julep, Jo Bell, and Buster. "Now that we have a working vocabulary for hieroglyphics, we need to figure out what to say." They all nodded and listened carefully. "In order to alert Tom to these crimes, the message needs to be short and . . ." She seemed to be looking for a word.

"Not sweet," Jo Bell offered.

"Exactly. Not sweet, but direct."

"How about 'murderers at large'?" Julep said.

"I'd say that's excessive," a voice outside the case intoned.

"Fatty! You're back!" Edith exclaimed.

"Oh, Fatty, you don't know what you missed," Jo Bell cried. "We saw the thief cutting a page and then Felix hopped into his pocket and —"

"I know it all, I saw it all, and now I bring you Felix."

"Felix!" Edith cried out.

"Get into that display case, Felix, and apologize to your mother this instant!" Fat Cat ordered.

Edith swung down from the web to embrace her errant son.

"I'm sorry, Mom," Felix said. "I really am. It was very foolish of me. I didn't mean to cause you worry."

"Oh, you gave my poor old heart a twitch, you did." She folded two of her legs beneath her cephalothorax and patted the region in the thorax where her heart was beating rapidly. "And I think my number ninety-five spigot port side seized up a bit. You know it always does when I get nervous."

Spiders have hundreds of microscopic spigots that are connected to their spinnerets. Each spinneret produces a unique silk for a specific purpose. Edith's number ninety-five spigot had a silk quite useful for frame building in web construction. It was this type of silk Edith had been counting on to construct hieroglyphs.

"Well, I'm back. So you don't have to worry about old ninety-five. But —" Felix looked up at Fatty, who was now plopped on top of the display case. "Can I tell them what we found out?"

"Yes, of course."

So Felix told them about what he'd overheard.

"A million dollars!" Jo Bell, Julep, and Buster kept repeating. But it was not the money that impressed Edith.

"These scoundrels were celebrating! They

were going to drink champagne, and you were in the champagne glass. You could have drowned, Felix." Edith began to sag.

"Steady there, old girl," Fatty said soothingly. "Your son is back. He's safe and there's work to be done."

"Yes, yes. Of course," Edith said. Her voice was still shaky, however. "Now, about the message. How much silk do you think we're going to have to put out?"

"That depends on what we want to say," Julep offered. "But I think we can use the silverfish. They are the perfect shape for forming some parts of the letters."

"True, true," Edith said as she reflected on the alphabet they had learned.

"If I may make a suggestion," Jo Bell said. "I think we should just say, 'Tom, go to *New World Explorers' Atlas* page 56 and the *Debrett's Fashion Portfolio* page 12.'"

"That's going to take a lot of silk," Edith said. "Not that I won't be up to it once I manage to relax old number ninety-five. But can we do a bit of editing?"

"Well, you can't cut out Tom's name. That's what's going to grab his attention," Julep said.

"Why don't we do a call number instead of a book title?" Jo Bell asked. "That will save a lot of words. What's the call number for that atlas with the map of New France?"

"G 995.1," Buster piped up.

"Yes," Jo Bell continued. "We just write 'Tom G 995.1.'"

"That's succinct," Edith said. "But do you think it's safe to write the call numbers as numerals?"

Buster tilted his head thoughtfully. "I think it all has to be in code."

"You're right, Buster. I don't think we can take any chances," Jo Bell agreed.

Much discussion followed: Would it take more silk to write out the call numbers or the title of the atlas and the fashion portfolio? Did they have to include the fashion portfolio? For as Buster said, many more maps had been stolen than fashion illustrations.

Finally, it was agreed that the message would be the name Tom with an exclamation mark and then the call numbers in hieroglyphs. Julep had not yet learned the system of hieroglyphic numerals, but Jo Bell immediately piped up. "I'm good in math. That can be my department."

*   *   *

And so they began that night. They worked in shifts. Edith and Felix went out to hunt for new silverfish and soon cleared out *Uncle Tom's Cabin*. Jo Bell and Buster, under Julep's direction, began the silken inscription.

It was Thursday night when they began. But because they had to make the hieroglyphs so big, they felt it would take them the entire weekend before the job was completed. They needed a sign that Tom couldn't miss.

SIXTEEN
⌒ Is for Tom

My, that's very interesting." It was Friday morning, and Tom Parker had made his usual stop at the spiders' display case. He was looking at what appeared to be a new web under construction by his favorite bug family in the Boston Public Library. This morning he was especially intrigued by the single silverfish that had been strung horizontally at the base of a shimmering arc of silk. There was a haunting familiarity to the design. "Now, what are you little guys up to?" he whispered.

"I don't appreciate him calling us 'little guys,'" Jo Bell said.

"Don't complain," Buster replied. "He's looking at it. He's realizing that this is something different."

"And it's just Friday," Julep said. "By Monday, we should have it almost done."

At noon they changed shifts. Felix devised a clever hauling net for their catch of silverfish. But it was still exhausting work. Edith sighed as she climbed back into the web. "I'm going to take a breather for a moment."

"Don't worry, Mom, I can haul these." Felix had become very attentive to his mother since his little escapade in Eldridge Montague's pocket.

"We almost have enough to finish the job, I think," Edith said. "We really cleaned out *Uncle Tom's Cabin*. I suggest that Jo Bell and Buster go to the prayer books, especially the Latin book of hours. There's one published in 1500, call number 242.9492. I saw a small gang heading in that direction."

"It shouldn't take that many more," Julep offered. "For the 'O' in 'Tom,' it's the quail symbol. One silverfish for the whole body should work."

"Yes," Edith said. "And I think we could use axial threads for the legs."

"How's your old ninety-five spigot, Mom?" asked Felix. "That's your axial silk one, isn't it?"

"It's kind of you to inquire, dear. I think it's all better. My silk flow seems fine."

A few hours later, shortly before the library closed, Tom came by the display case again. His mouth dropped open. He whispered the name of the first glyph for the "T," then the second for the "O." *Could it be?* he thought. Could it possibly be that the spider family was trying to communicate with him? He'd felt a special bond with this little family ever since they'd arrived. What were they trying to tell him?

"Good night, Tom," Rosemary said as she got up from her desk to leave. "Have a nice week-end down on the Cape."

"Yes, I will," he said distractedly.

"See you on Tuesday, right? Are you still taking an extra day?"

"Yes," he said. And at the moment, he very much regretted it. Tom knew he ought to leave right away to beat the traffic down to Cape Cod, but he decided to stay just a bit longer. *They*

seem so intent, he thought as he watched the five spiders working away with incredible industry, not paying the least bit of attention to him. There was almost a desperation to their spinning and weaving.

An hour later, Tom was stuck in traffic on Route 3, in somewhat of a daze. *It's simply unbelievable*, he thought for the one hundredth time. The spiders had spelled his name. At five forty-five, the largest of the spider children, the one he thought was a girl, although it was hard to be sure, had completed the glyph for the letter "M." The last letter in his name.

The image was burnished in his mind's eye. It was an owl, elegantly constructed with a large gleaming silverfish slanted at just the right angle and a smaller one placed for each foot. The rest of the body was woven with silk thread. It was a work of art. Tom could picture it now even as evening fell, car lights blazed, and impatient drivers honked their horns as if the sound alone would blast them down Route 3 and across the Sagamore Bridge to the Cape.

The temperature was hovering — even at this hour — near 90, and everyone was thinking of the beach except Tom Parker. He was tempted to make a U-turn and drive straight back to Boston, but how would he explain it to his aging mother? He had not been to visit her for almost a month. No, he had to continue. *I mean*, he thought, *what would I say? "Mom, I had to go back to work because some brown recluse spiders are trying to send me a message."* It would sound certifiably crazy. He'd be packed off to the loony bin.

Meanwhile, back in the Rare Books Department, Jo Bell was directing the beginning of the first hieroglyphic call numbers. Silverfish lent themselves well to the hieroglyphic numbering system because the numbers one through ten were shown as groupings of short lines. It was, however, a somewhat complex engineering job. She and Buster had spun a double-strand halyard for hoisting the silverfish that would be used for several of the call numbers.

"All right, commence hoist!" She barked out the command. A glimmering silverfish rose on the halyard.

"Halt and begin to pay out!"

Julep and Felix swung out on a radial and began to squeeze out number four sticky thread.

"Attachment complete!" Felix called down to Jo Bell. "Over and out!"

The silverfish now hung in the web. Soon they would begin the next set of call numbers for the *New World Explorers' Atlas* and be one step closer to catching the thieves.

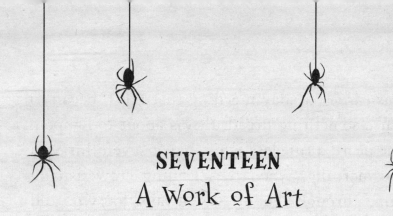

SEVENTEEN
A Work of Art

On Sunday night, one minute before midnight, Edith and the children had completed the job.

"It's a work of art!" Fatty exclaimed, gazing at the shimmering threads that showed the complicated hieroglyph numbers.

They couldn't wait until Tom returned.

But by nine forty-five on Monday, when there was still no sign of the conservator, they began to worry.

"He's never late," Buster said. "I hope he didn't have an accident driving down to the Cape."

"Surely we would have heard," Edith replied. "Rosemary would have said something."

They waited for Tom all day Monday. But it

was early Tuesday morning that Edith began to sense something dreadful was about to happen. She heard a tuneless whistling at seven thirty in the morning, when the cleaning crew usually came through. But it was always Joe who did the sweeping and dusting in the rare books room, and he never whistled. The whistling was coming closer and closer, and suddenly there was a creaking noise that sent a jolt from Edith's fangs to her spinnerets.

Edith heard a scream. She was not sure if it came from herself or one of her children. Then Felix shouted, "SCATTER AND DIVE FOR COVER!"

The case was opening. An immense feather duster hovered like a dreadful cloud above them.

"Climb!" cried Edith. "Get out of the web." And then it was all gone, every fantastic filament, every last shred of the hieroglyphs they had spent three whole days weaving.

Next, there was a terrible roar as the cleaning lady poked something with a nozzle into the corner of the case. "Outta here! We'll be sucked up!" Felix cried out. Draglines flew through the air so they could haul themselves out of the display and escape the great sucking mechanical beast that had invaded their peaceful domain.

"Well, that's done," the cleaning woman said. "What a mess! Bet no one dusted that in years! These librarians and their books. So dirty!"

Edith was trembling. She still didn't know if her children had escaped or had been vacuumed up. "Children!" Edith called.

"Jo Bell?"

"Here!"

"Felix?"

"Here, Mom."

"Julep?" She waited. "Julep?" Panic was rising. "Julep, darling, Julep!"

"Oh, for the love of Pete!" they heard the cleaning lady exclaim. "Yikes, it's a spider!"

Edith's tiny heart beat wildly, but her body was frozen with fear. Her youngest child could be killed or could be scared into biting the cleaning lady. That, too, would spell certain doom for them all.

Four seconds later, there was the softest little noise on the surface of the display case. A noise so tiny that only a spider could have felt the vibrations.

"It's Julep," Jo Bell said. "Julep!"

"Is she alive?" Edith croaked, hiding her eyes behind one of her eight legs.

"Of course I'm alive. She just flicked me off her."

"Oh! Thank heavens." And with that, Edith collapsed.

"What happened? What happened?" Buster had been sleeping across the room somewhere in a boxed set of nineteenth-century locomotive drawings. "I heard a noise. It sounded like a vacuum cleaner."

"It was!" Jo Bell said somberly.

Buster looked around the case and staggered a bit. It felt as if his eight eyes were spinning. "But everything's gone. The webs, the message. It's all gone!"

Indeed the shimmering hieroglyphs were gone. The display case had not a speck of dust, and the glass was polished on both sides and gleaming. Even the precious book of the Liang dynasty sparkled with a new cleanliness.

"I hate hygiene!" Edith said in a low rumbling voice that the children had never before heard.

But the spiders' devastation was nothing compared to that of Tom Parker. Five minutes after the cleaning lady went on her merry hygienic way, Tom arrived. He didn't bother to take off his jacket but walked directly over to the case. He looked down through the glass and blinked. Then, emitting a small gasp, he pulled out his reading glasses and bent down for a closer look. "It's gone." He blinked several times. He looked up and, with a confused gaze, stared into the perpetual twilight of the rare books room. "Did I dream it?"

"No! No! No!" the spiders all cried out together. But Tom could not hear their melancholy vibrations.

He turned to Rosemary, who had just arrived. "Rosemary, isn't Monday the cleaning day for rare books?"

"Yes, but Joe has been out, and I think someone else came up this morning instead."

"Indeed they did. The display case was opened."

"Was something stolen?" Rosemary asked, jumping up from her desk.

"No, dusted."

"Oh, dear. I know you don't like that case dusted. I should have put a note on it. But I'll be sure to call Custodial Services and tell them not to dust the case again if Joe is going to be out longer."

"It's too late," Tom whispered to himself. "Too late."

EIGHTEEN
It's Never Too late

"It's never too late, Tom! It's never too late!" Jo Bell had swung up to the top of the display case and was shouting at him through the glass.

"He can't hear you, Jo Bell. He doesn't speak spider," Julep called up at her.

"It's useless, Jo Bell," Felix said.

"We're beaten," Edith nearly sobbed.

"Mom!" Jo Bell glared at her mother. "How can you say that? You never talk that way. We need to think of something!"

Jo Bell slid down her dragline to pace the felt floor of the display case. Her head was tipped down. She found the spotlessness of the freshly vacuumed felt offensive. *There's not a speck of dust! This is no way to live!*

But Jo Bell would not let herself or her family be defeated. No idiot human with a vacuum was going to stand in the way of justice.

Jo Bell turned to Buster, her mom, her brother, and her sister. They all seemed to be waiting for her to say something. They were all paying full attention.

"Listen to me." Her six eyes were smoldering. "This is not an end. This is a beginning."

"What do you mean?" asked Felix.

"Just that we've been defeated in the display case. But we shall rebuild our web with the hieroglyphic code. And we shall do it not only here. We shall send out our message far and wide. We shall

weave it in the case, on the shelves, in the stacks, and right across Tom Parker's desk. The dusting is finished. The cleaners don't come back for a week. And in that time, we shall fight on."

Suddenly, the spiders felt a fluttering in their spinnerets. "Bestir yourself," Jo Bell continued. "There is silk to be made! We will weave on and defend the volumes of this library against the tyranny of unchecked greed, against the violence of the X-ACTO blade. We shall spin on with growing confidence, for we have done it once before and shall do it again. And we shall grow bolder in the air! We shall not be defeated and we shall never surrender. Tom Parker will see and understand our message and step forth to rescue what rightfully belongs to the citizens of this fair city!"

A stunned silence followed this speech. But no one was more stunned than Jo Bell herself. Her siblings and her mother were looking at her in awe. Moments before, they had been awash with disappointment and anger, exhausted from their efforts. But now their spigots itched to unleash new silk.

"Allons, enfants!" Jo Bell had slipped into the first words of the French national anthem without realizing it. But she quickly switched back to English. "Let's go, spiders of the Boston Public Library. Onward!"

"I know where there is a new batch of silverfish!" Julep said.

"I can start making the two-strand hoist," Buster offered.

"And I can set one up on the shelf where the *Wurmach Encyclopedia of Hieroglyphs* is," Felix said.

The five spiders had never worked so hard. But it seemed easier. They were able to spin out the hieroglyphic words faster, more smoothly. It was as if their spinnerets had been greased, for the silk just flowed. And not once did anyone complain.

When dawn began to break on Wednesday, they all straggled back to the display case. Four different webs had been woven in places that Tom would never miss — beginning with the computer on his own desk.

"What's this?" Tom whispered. Stretched across the computer screen and anchored on either side of the keyboard was a message that sent chills up his spine.

He rushed to the display case, where he saw the same message repeated. He leaned forward and breathed heavily over the case.

"Tom, are you all right?" Rosemary asked.

"Yes, yes. Just fine."

"There's a fellow on the phone about the *Wurmach Encyclopedia* again. He'll be in later this morning. I have to go down to that meeting in the trustees' room. I'll be back in an hour, but I can get the Wurmach now," Rosemary said.

"Wait! I'll get it!" Tom answered.

Tom Parker had a sudden instinct, a hunch like a sixth sense. He raced into the stacks where the early dictionaries and encyclopedias were kept, and he was right. Here stretched the biggest web of all. This time, there were three simple words spelled in enormous glyphs:

"Smoot and Montague, those scoundrels!" shouted Tom.

The children and Edith had followed Tom as he raced to the three sites where they had constructed webs.

"He got it!" Felix cried out. Then they began to dance a celebratory jig.

"Oh!" sighed Edith. "I am so proud of all of you children. It won't be long now!"

"You can call it spiderwebs," Buster said. "But it's truly a dragnet — and it's Jo Bell's. What

a brilliant idea, Jo Bell." He couldn't conceal his admiration.

"But if it hadn't been for Julep, none of us could have learned hieroglyphics. And" — Jo Bell paused — "if it hadn't been for Felix, I would never have thought of the double-strand hoist."

"Mission accomplished!" Felix said, and gave a snappy little salute with his pedipalps, his two forelegs.

"Well, not quite accomplished," Edith cautioned. "When the thread on the dragnet is pulled tight and the vandals ensnared, then we can truly say mission accomplished." Edith turned to Jo Bell with gleaming eyes. "Thank you, dear," she said.

All five spiders had the same image in their minds: Agnes Smoot and Eldridge Montague ensnared in the sticky threads of a great big web with two spiderish cops arriving to haul them to jail.

NINETEEN
Things Get Nasty

After his quick translation of the call numbers, Tom Parker went immediately to the map section and then to the fashion journals. He felt weak when he saw the damage. In their haste, the vandals had destroyed binding threads and spines of the books. Beautiful pages of maps and fashion drawings were gone. Tom had to sit down, right down on the floor. *This might only be the beginning,* he thought. He had to act.

He took the two violated books and, cradling them in his arms, ran down to the first floor and across the courtyard to the library trustees' room. He burst in just as the trustees were taking a vote on cutting funding to the branch libraries.

"I am sorry to interrupt, but I'm here to show you another kind of cutting!"

A stunned silence enveloped the room as Tom lay the books on the table in front of the members of the board.

"I can't believe it!" Buster gasped.

"Believe what?" Edith asked. Edith and her kids had retired to the display case to wait for Tom's return.

"They're back!"

"Who?" Jo Bell asked. "Tom and the police?"

"No. Them! Eldridge and Agnes. Rosemary is fetching them both books right now!"

Four minutes later, all the spiders were casting draglines through the air and scrambling toward the desk where Eldridge sat with yet another antique atlas. It contained priceless maps from the sixteenth century, showing the spice trade routes. They watched in horror as Eldridge took out his blade.

Suddenly, a voice rang out. "How you got that blade in here, I'll never know. But I insist that you drop it right this moment."

"It's Tom! He's back!" Jo Bell cried.

"Thank heavens!" said Edith.

The spiders' exclamations of relief and joy set the air buzzing. Every hair on their bodies seemed to reverberate.

"There must be some mistake!" Eldridge Montague protested.

"There's no mistake," said Tom. "Now drop it."

They heard the X-ACTO blade hit the floor.

"Great silk!" Edith exclaimed. "Look who's here!"

It was Agnes Smoot, and she was not carrying a blade but a huge book raised above her head. Her intentions were clear. She was going to slam it down on poor Tom's head. And there was no other human being in the room. Rosemary had gone off to fetch a book for Agnes.

"What are we to do?" Edith said in a hysterical pitch that seemed to defy the laws of vibration.

Jo Bell did not even think. She cast her dragline and landed squarely in the middle of Agnes Smoot's wig. She began to crawl down Agnes's bangs and leapt onto the rim of her glasses. It was an act of stunning courage, for Jo Bell knew that Felix had lost a leg the only time he confronted a human. But this woman was creeping

up on Tom with a fat book that could knock him senseless, and Jo Bell couldn't simply stand aside.

A second later, Buster landed by her side. "Venom! Use your venom, Jo Bell!"

"I can't!" Jo Bell cried.

A sudden terrible scream tore the air. Jo Bell felt as though she were falling, falling . . . falling. But it was Agnes Smoot who was falling. Her eyes crossed crazily as she looked up at Jo Bell dangling on the bridge of her glasses.

"BROWN RECLUSE!" she shrieked.

The glasses and the book all went tumbling to the floor. Tom turned around and, seeing how narrowly he had escaped being clobbered by a five-pound book, grew deathly pale.

"Don't faint now!" Jo Bell screamed.

And although he didn't speak spider, Tom seemed to understand. The next thing she knew, he was racing to his desk to hit the emergency button.

And then it was over.

TWENTY
A Last Webtime Story

The next morning, the *Boston Globe* headlines screamed:

VANDALS AND VERMIN INFEST
RARE BOOKS ROOM OF BPL!

At ten that morning, Tom Parker held a press conference.

"Is it true, Mr. Parker, that the suspect claims she was about to be attacked by a brown recluse spider, and that's why she carried an X-ACTO blade?"

"An X-ACTO blade for a spider? C'mon, sir. Why not a can of insecticide? It's not true." Tom turned to face the TV cameras. "What is true is that Agnes Smoot — and we now know her real name is Diane de Funk — and her husband, Eldridge Montague, are thieves who thought nothing of cutting up priceless books, treasures of the Boston Public Library. The public has been robbed. No more questions, ladies and gentlemen."

Tom went to his office and sat at his desk. The wonderful web still stretched across the computer screen. The five spiders had arranged themselves in a neat row on the top edge of the screen. "Oh, my goodness," he whispered, overwhelmed with emotion at the sight of these tiny heroes.

At that moment, the telephone rang.

"Yes, President Wilkins." He paused. His face went white. "Tomorrow morning . . . so soon? Do you really feel this is necessary?" There was a long pause. "But . . . but . . . Yes, Mr. President. I'll put up a notice. The Rare Books Department will be sealed off. Closed. I realize . . . quite toxic. I'll tell my staff not to come in for three days until the air clears."

Not again! mourned Edith.

"Good-bye, President Wilkins." Tom wanted to slam down the telephone, but for fear of jiggling the marvelous web, he set it down softly.

Tom took off his glasses. Tears were streaming down his cheeks. "I know that I cannot understand your language, but somehow you understand mine. I think you know that this is farewell. The city sanitation department insists on sending an extermination team tomorrow." He sighed. "Public safety, they say. If they only knew!"

Tom wiped his eyes, put on his glasses again, hit a button on his keyboard, and began to type. The screen soon pulsed with colorful pictures.

"Farewell, my friends," Julep translated. "That's what he wrote." She turned to Edith. "Mom, he was our first human friend and now we're losing him."

Edith was not sure how to answer, but all the children were looking to her. "Do you remember, children, when we first arrived here at the Boston Public Library, and Tom welcomed us so warmly? Do you remember what you asked, Julep?"

"I asked if this was the Place Where Time Has Stopped. The place where spiders can live in the open and never be afraid of humans. Where no humans are ever afraid of us, and there are no E-Men, like the exterminators who are coming tomorrow."

Buster felt something quicken in his spinnerets. He had been waiting a long time to hear the story of the Place Where Time Has Stopped.

"Right, and what did I answer?"

"You said" — Julep's voice grew very tiny — "that this was not the Place Where Time Has

Stopped, but you thought we were getting closer."

"Yes. I truly believe that. It is our destiny, but before we reach that place, we must endure some travails."

"What are travails?" asked Julep.

"Hard and sometimes painful times," Edith replied.

"Enough already!" Felix blurted out. "I already lost one leg, remember. I might not be able to regrow it again if I lose another. I'm heavy in the travails department."

"We'll get there. I have faith. Faith in all of you. Children, you are brave, inventive, honest, and so smart."

Does she mean me, too? Buster wondered.

"So I think this evening it would be appropriate if our webtime story was 'The Story of the Place Where Time Has Stopped.' For it is a story of hope."

Edith tucked her fangs in neatly and, settling herself into a corner of the web, began to speak in that somewhat hazy webtime story voice that seemed to come from gauzy blue mists of time.

"There is a place far, far away. Some say it is a grand mansion, some say it is a small cabin in the woods, some say it is across an ocean," Edith began. Buster looked over at the three young spiders. He could see that they knew this story so well that they were repeating every word silently to themselves. Oh, he was envious of them. All he knew were words from books. No one had ever told him a story like this one. What would he do when they left? It was hard to imagine life without them! He closed his eyes and listened on.

EPILOGUE

And so I don't know how to put it." Buster sighed. "But my life has never been as complete as when you and your family arrived here at the Boston Public Library."

Jo Bell considered as Buster finished his little speech. Of course she wanted him to come along, but she couldn't help but remember how he had shouted, "Venom! Use your venom, Jo Bell!" The words had haunted her.

Ever since that fateful moment on Agnes Smoot's bangs, she had asked herself if Buster really liked her. Liked her for herself and not just her venom. She looked at him now almost shyly, with only three of her six eyes. *What if he just wants a crime buster and not a friend — not a girl friend?* She took a deep breath and began to speak.

"I realize you have to leave, too. But do you want to come with us?" Jo Bell stammered out the question.

"Oh, Jo Bell!" It was Edith, peeking around the corner of a web at the other end of the display case where Buster and Jo Bell were talking. "I think that's a wonderful idea. Buster is part of the family now."

"Yes, yes, but, Mom, could I have a few minutes alone with Buster? I need to ask him something — something private."

"Of course, dear."

As soon as Edith left, Buster blurted out, "Something private? What, Jo Bell? What?"

"Well, perhaps 'personal' is a better word."

"What is it?"

"Look, this is difficult for me to say. But do you like me for me, and not just for . . . well, you know, my venom?"

Buster looked confused.

Yikes, boys are stupid! thought Jo Bell.

She took a deep breath. "I want a real friend-ship, not just to be your partner in solving crimes. I want a real friend, Buster. I have a mom, a sister, a brother, but I still need a plain, wonderful friend."

"How could you think it was just your fangs?" Buster gasped. "You thought up the whole idea of the hieroglyphics and the dragnet. You were the mastermind and you did it without fangs or venom. You . . . you . . ."

Oh, he wished he could think of something wonderful to say to her. How awful that she had thought this. He cursed himself for every time — and there were far too many — when he had said the word "venom." Then it came to him. Once when he was very young, he had dropped in at story time in the children's department. A story about a spider and a pig by a very famous writer was being read aloud. He remembered that story and the beautiful sentences that the author created with such simple words.

He began in a shaky voice, "Jo Bell, I have something to say. Forgive me if the words are not my own, and a bit turned around. But, Jo Bell, you are terrific, you are radiant, you are brilliant, you are some spider!"

Jo Bell's tiny little heart skipped a beat. "I'll tell Mom! We meet Fatty in ten minutes at the corner of Dartmouth and Boylston. Be there!"

Then all the silk in the display case webs began to shake and shimmer as Edith, Felix, and Julep bounced up and down on the threads. "He's coming. He's coming!" they shouted.

"Talk about spying!" Jo Bell said with a laugh. "Is there no privacy around here?"

"A new member of the family!" Edith rejoiced.

"Another boy spider at last!" Felix sang.

"I have a new brother!" Julep cried out gleefully.

"And I have a friend," Jo Bell said softly. "A real friend."

AUTHOR'S NOTE

Many things in this book are true, others aren't, and some are halfway between.

As I'm sure you know, real spiders don't use words to talk. Nor do they read, nor do they wear hats as in Stephen Gilpin's wonderful illustrations. But here are a few things that are true about brown recluse spiders.

* Spiders have multiple eyes — usually eight (except for brown recluses, which have only six). In spite of all these eyes, spiders do not see well.

* Spiders DO receive a lot of information through their ability to pick up vibrations.

* The tiny hairs on their legs work like motion detectors and alert them to the smallest movements.

* Spider blood is blue. This is because spider blood, unlike human blood, contains copper.
* Brown recluse spiderwebs look slightly blue.
* Spiders can regrow lost legs if they are still fairly young.
* Spider silk is much stronger than any rope or even steel cable that humans make.
* Finally, it's true that brown recluse spiders, like Edith and her three children, are very shy. But they can be very dangerous if they do bite. Their venom is toxic and causes necrotic wounds, which means that their bite causes human flesh to die. In some cases, brown recluse spider bites can be fatal. So enjoy reading about brown recluse spiders, but please — DON'T PLAY WITH THEM!

Now for the halfway-between things. The Boston Public Library is a real place. It was the very first public library in America, and it is considered a national treasure because of its beautiful architecture and its wonderful collection of books. It is true that the personal library of

John Adams, our second president, can be found at this library in the Rare Books Department, which is in fact located on the third floor. President Adams's books are kept on a mezzanine level of the lobby of the rare books room.

In 2003 there was an extensive exhibit at the library of books with movable parts, or as they are more commonly known, pop-up books. But the library itself does not own many of these books.

Several of the titles of other books mentioned I have made up, such as *Les Dessins des Hauts Couturiers*, the *Wurmach Encyclopedia of Hieroglyphs*, and the *New World Explorers' Atlas*.

Many books, however, really are to be found at the Boston Public Library such as a first edition of *Uncle Tom's Cabin*, as well as the popular nineteenth-century magazine *Alexander's Weekly Messenger*. There is also a forensic map and a copy of the famous Paul Revere engraving of the Boston Massacre that Adams used in his defense of the British soldiers.

Also, in 2006 an antiquarian map collector and expert named Edward Forbes Smiley was found guilty and sentenced to jail for stealing over ninety-seven maps valued at more than three million dollars from various libraries including the Boston Public Library. His instrument of choice was an X-ACTO knife, but he was also known to use dental floss for the removal of some of the maps

Kathryn Lasky is author of the bestselling Guardians of Ga'Hoole series, which has sold more than 4 million copies worldwide. Her newest books include The Deadlies Book 1: *Felix Takes the Stage*, and the Wolves of the Beyond and Daughters of the Sea series. Kathryn's books have received a Newbery Honor, a Boston Globe–Horn Book Award, and a Washington Post–Children's Book Guild Award. She lives with her husband in Cambridge, Massachusetts.